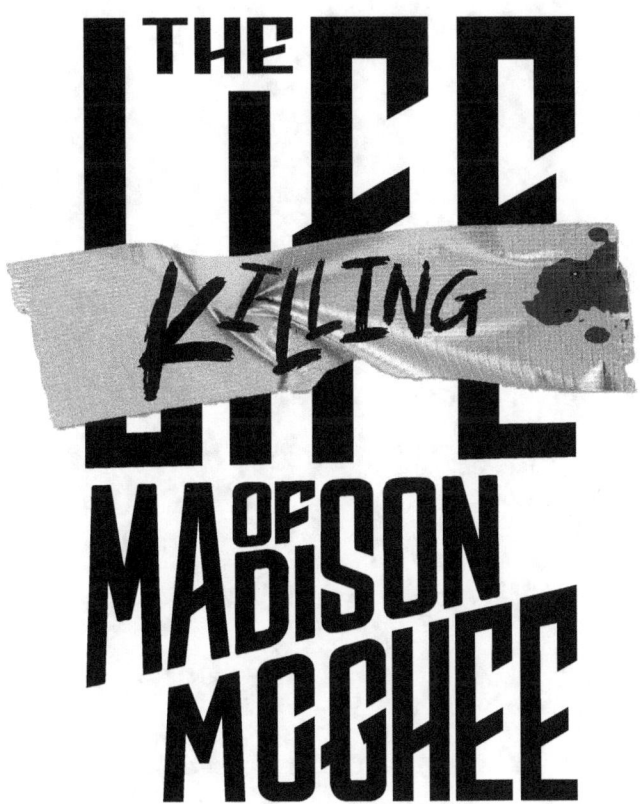

THE LIFE KILLING OF MADISON MCGHEE

THE LIFE KILLING OF MADISON MCGHEE

B. DANIELLE WATKINS

Halo
PUBLISHING
INTERNATIONAL

PUBLISHING
INTERNATIONAL

Halo Publishing International
7550 W IH-10 #800, PMB 2069,
San Antonio, TX 78229

First Edition, September 2024
ISBN: 978-1-63765-637-2
Library of Congress Control Number: 2024911976

Halo Publishing International is a self-publishing company that publishes adult fiction and non-fiction, children's literature, self-help, spiritual, and faith-based books. We continually strive to help authors reach their publishing goals and provide many different services that help them do so. We do not publish books that are deemed to be politically, religiously, or socially disrespectful, or books that are sexually provocative, including erotica. Halo reserves the right to refuse publication of any manuscript if it is deemed not to be in line with our principles. Do you have a book idea you would like us to consider publishing? Please visit www.halopublishing.com for more information.

This novel was supported in part by the
Barb Seegert Memorial Art Grant in Decatur, Georgia.

This grant seeks to help lesbian women under forty
in their pursuit of the arts.

For more information, please email
lezartgrant@gmail.com.

This novel belongs to every *Goosebumps* fan turned *True Crime* head who remembers the *Choose Your Own Adventure* book debuts in the '90s. The fun of feeling as if you are telling the story yourself and choosing the ending that makes sense to you.

Right, wrong, or indifferent—we had hours of fun trying to figure it out.

I pray this novel brings you the same joy, in an adult sense, and you are able to figure out who killed Madison McGhee. If not, have fun failing...and trying again.

This is a hell of a way for you to start your first case. They threw you right in, didn't they? Vaseline clearly wasn't even an option! Crass, I know, but you will learn soon, in our line of work, sugar coatings don't last long.

Nice to meet you, by the way. I'm Detective Abigail Shank, and I'm the lead homicide investigator around these parts. New York City isn't what it was when I was coming up through the ranks. Now, people are nasty, and the crimes, these days you have to have a real stomach for this stuff. I'm sure, when this is all over, one of two things will be true: you will be a damn-good detective, or you will be back on the streets faster than they can call me MAMA!

Enough of the small talk—we need to talk about this case. The first thing you need to know: this isn't a slam-dunk case. For some murders, we have our suspect, our murder weapon, and things are in our favor. That is not this case.

The second thing you need to know: you cannot believe every innocent face, and every eye that sheds tears isn't sad. If you're going to make it around here, throw your sympathy out the door and pay attention.

Lastly, you can't even trust yourself. Your gut has no discernment. We stick to the facts and the evidence; we don't have time for hunches, psychics, voodoo queens, or late-night dreams.

Do you understand? Excellent. Let's get right into it.

On Thursday, March 17, around 2:45 a.m., we got a call here at the station. We found it odd because the call did not come through 911. The call came directly to my office, and the caller, who remained anonymous, said we may want to head to the 700 block of 154th Street.

To be clear, our office doesn't usually deal directly with calls like this, but something about this call was different. It didn't sit well with the receptionist, so she asked more questions.

"What's going on, ma'am?" she asked though she was unsure if it was a man or woman on the phone, but she had to say something.

"She's dead."

"Who is she?"

"Madison McGhee."

The receptionist held the phone for a moment and then got my attention. "How did Madison die?"

"I killed her."

I immediately dispatched some detectives to the scene, and I implored Jackie—my receptionist, in case you didn't catch on—to keep this person on the phone.

"Are you in danger, ma'am?" Jackie was cautious as we tried to track the call to send a few beat cops to the location.

"Not anymore."

"Were you hurt?"

"No." There were moments of silence on the phone. The caller was breathing really weirdly; it was some odd shit!

We had the folks here in the office tracing the call, but they kept failing.

Jackie sat on the phone for a few more moments, playing the silent game, and then looked at me. "What now?" she whispered.

I took the phone from her because I figured maybe, if somebody with a little more authority in their voice started talking, she or he may respond differently. "This is Detective Shank."

"She's dead, Detective."

"And you killed her?"

"Yes."

"Why?"

"You'll see."

"What is there for me to see?"

"You'll see." Then the line went dead.

Jackie and I looked at each other. I grabbed my keys and headed to the scene.

My entire ride to the scene, all I kept thinking about was the "you'll see" and how it made the hairs on the back of my neck stand up. There is nothing more sinister than a self-righteous murderer. The amount of gall it takes...and the precision. We never traced the call. We had nothing but the voice on the line; we didn't even know if we were responding to a real call. But I will never forget the feeling I had when I hung up the phone.

As I approached the 700 block of 154th Street, I saw the crime tape and red and blue lights; I eliminated the possibility it was a prank call. Madison McGhee must be dead.

I got out of my cruiser and walked under the tape. Immediately a deputy began to brief me.

"What do we have, Clark?"

"It's pretty gruesome, ma'am."

"What the hell does that mean, Clark?" I was already annoyed.

Clark is a new guy, but not like you, new guy. Clark just started the beat about a month ago. Fresh out of the academy, and he is wet behind the ears. Squeamish as hell! Everything is gruesome to him. A damn paper cut is gruesome to him!

Anyways, I digress.

"It's a homicide, ma'am," Clark started. "African American female, looks to be in her late twenties, but could be in her thirties. Black women age differently than White women."

"Focus, Clark."

"Yes, ma'am. When we arrived on the scene, the victim was lying in the middle of the street, blood streaming under her body. The blood had been running for so long it had made it to the curb and started running down the gutter. Looks like she was shot and stabbed. Could be a crime of passion, but we aren't sure. There is no weapon in the immediate area."

Clark and I approached the victim who was, in fact, lying in the middle of the street. At first look, she could have been beaten; there was blood all over her face. But upon further examination, I noticed that the blood on her face seemed to be spatter from the knife entering and exiting her body, spraying blood everywhere.

The victim's eyes were open, and it was as if she were looking right at me. This was different too. Most cases, the person is dead, and there is no life left in the eyes. But not Madison. Madison's eyes still had hope, without life, and that was bone chilling. What was the last thing she saw, and who hated her so much as to leave her in the street looking like this?

There were two bullet-entry points. One in her abdominal area and the other in her left shoulder. The knife wounds, to the naked eye, seemed to number easily over fifteen. This girl was stabbed everywhere on her body and left in the middle of the street to bleed to death, and then she was shot twice to make sure the job was done correctly. I have been a detective a very long time, and a cop even longer, but I have never seen anything like this.

There was no one around; the area was silent, but the scene spoke of a violence and cruelty so severe that someone had to have heard the murder. I started walking around the perimeter to see if I could find anything, at least some identification to determine who she was. The caller had told us the victim's name was Madison McGhee, but we hadn't verified that yet.

The victim's body was half dressed. On her torso was only a bra; she had on a pair of ripped jeans, soaked in blood, so their true color was unknown, a sock on her right foot, and a sock and sneaker on her left, but the sneaker was untied.

On the curb, one of the other deputies found a wallet. "Ma'am, this wallet was lying here, and it had no blood or anything on it. We are going to take it in to be printed."

"Any ID?"

"Madison Melissa McGhee. Thirty-five years old. Lives just up the way in the 800 block."

The initial major red flag for me: Why was Madison a block away from her home, half dressed? Was she being chased? Did she run here? Was she dropped off here?

You see, Rookie—if I may call you that—these are the questions you have to ask yourself when you're out here in the field. You have to have your third eye open at all times, you have to think like a criminal, you have to think like a victim, and then you have to think like a detective. You have to do it all at once. You can't miss anything!

I started walking down the block; I needed to trace what could have been Madison's last steps. I needed to keep an eye out for anything that could have been left in the street. About 500 feet from where she was found, there was a trickle of blood, but it wasn't consistent. So I started looking around for bullet casings, but there was nothing. The closer I got to her house, the more I felt that the crime scene was right where Madison lay.

The ideal situation would be to start canvasing the area right away. Find witnesses, get statements from neighbors, see if they have any cameras on their properties. I needed to gain ground in the investigation, but at this point, it was almost four in the morning.

I knocked on a few doors, but didn't get an answer. That was when things got interesting.

CSI arrived and locked down the scene. I noticed a few cars slow to see what was going on, but the deputies on the scene kept the onlookers at bay. I could hear faint crying in the distance, so I walked over to the crime tape to see what was going on.

"What happened to my sister?" a woman later identified as Miranda struggled to get out through her tears.

Red flag number two: We hadn't called anybody. How did this woman know something happened to Madison?

"Ma'am, who are you?" I asked.

"She's her fucking sister! Didn't you hear her?"

"And you are?"

"Aubrey." Aubrey began to break down as she continued, "Miranda's wife and Madison's sister-in-law."

"I'm sorry for your loss, both of you. But I have to ask—how did you know to come here?"

Before they could answer, we heard a yell come from another car as a man came jumping out of it in the most dramatic fashion imaginable. When I say dramatic, I mean he was RuPaul, Billy Porter, and Robin Williams from *The Birdcage*, all in one.

You do know the movie *The Birdcage*, right? At least familiar with the play? Kids! It's good shit! Watch it!

Anyways, he bounced his flamboyantly devastated ass up to the tape and then collapsed crying.

Miranda stopped for a second and looked at him in confusion as Aubrey helped him up.

"Get up, Ten," Aubrey mumbled under her breath.

"Sir, and you are..."

"Lawd, not Madison. Jesus! Why, Lawwwwwwwwwwwd?" Ten screamed and then fell back to the ground, almost taking Aubrey with him.

"Her assistant," Miranda whispered.

"Why did they do it, Lawd!?"

"Shut the hell up!" a woman said as she walked up.

Ten immediately stopped crying and stood up as the woman adjusted her position to avoid seeing the body just a few feet away from her.

"Ma'am," I finally got out, "who are you?"

"Dr. Dimitria Kincaid." Dr. Kincaid reached out to shake my hand. "I'm Ten's and Madison's therapist."

Now, I am standing there and looking at Madison's sister, sister-in-law, assistant, and shrink, and not one person has told me how they all knew to come to this location at this moment in the middle of the night to see if Madison in fact had been murdered.

"Can someone tell me how you all knew to come here?"

"I got a call," Dr Kincaid stated as a single tear streamed down her face.

"I did too," Aubrey chimed in.

"Me too," Miranda whispered.

"Me too. God, just take me now!" Ten screamed.

"Do you know who it was that called you?" My gut told me it was the same person who had called me, but as I already told you, we aren't trusting guts around here.

There was no answer. They all stood there, looked at each other, and then back at me.

"Hello...?"

"I never heard the voice before," Miranda whispered. "They called me several times from an unknown number, and when I answered, they said my sister was dead. They said to come to the 700 block of her street, and this is what I saw when I got here." Miranda lost it completely in that moment.

I don't have siblings, but I've seen enough families shattered by murder, and I felt her pain through her words. Of the four people standing in front of me with the same information I got, she was the most distraught. Ten gave an Academy-award-winning performance, but nothing like Miranda. I took note of that.

Aubrey seemed to be attempting to be strong for Miranda, but I kept catching her glancing at Madison's body. Her glances caught my attention because they weren't that of a mourning sister-in-law. She had some malice in her eyes, but when she saw Miranda's grief, she softened. That was interesting to me.

Ten was so damn dramatic. I started to cuff him, but then I figured he might like that. The dramatics were alarming—an assistant so torn up because their boss was dead. I don't know about you, but I know if somebody knocked me off, Jackie might have a party! I'm just telling you what I know. Ten's performance was curious, but I had to take into consideration the condition of the body and the disturbing phone call in the middle of the night from a stranger. I'm sure that could make even the most reserved person a tad dramatic.

Dr. Kincaid kept her composure. I expected as much from a therapist. They are trained to hide emotions. Tears streamed down her face steadily as she kept her back to the body and attempted to calm Ten down. Attempted, because she didn't do shit. He was waking up the neighbors with all his hollering and carrying on. Her energy was cold, but I imagine at that point all our energies were cold.

I asked them all to go down to the station to give official statements; they would have to wait for me while I spoke with the awakening neighborhood. They all agreed and departed from the scene as I got the details on who Madison Melissa McGhee, aged thirty-five, really was.

Madison McGhee, born and raised in Yonkers, New York. If you know anything about a girl from Yonkers, you know she is about getting the bag! She came from a modest family; her older sister, Miranda, was the golden child until she wasn't.

Madison stood out in sports, academics, looks...everything. The sisters were both beautiful unit, but Madison had the personality to go with it. Madison was the shit! That's just the reality of it. She graduated high school at the age of sixteen as the valedictorian and then headed on down to Manhattan to NYU to study law. She finished law school at twenty-three, passed the bar, and immediately started working toward opening her own firm—McGhee and Associates. You know, the big glass building down on Forty-Sixth? Yeah, that's her firm. She built a reputation as a powerhouse in the courtroom, as well as in her life. Biggest dyke on the block. She had taken 'em down, left, right, and up! I hate I didn't know her.

But you know what comes with that type of power, don't you? Mo' money, mo' problems. Ask Sean Combs; I've got his file on my damn desk right now. It makes my head hurt! A few years back, some girl sued Madison for sexual assault or harassment—I can't remember now which one it was—but it was one of those things that you really don't want to be associated with.

It hit her hard, and just as the pandemic was coming into play, it was about to ruin her. Then, all of a sudden, it went away. Just like COVID. I'm not sure of all the details. I don't work with living-people issues; I deal with the dead. But what I do know is that if Madison did everything she was accused of doing, that shit wouldn't have gone away.

After that, Madison seems to have been just building up her second business, an advertising agency. Know that glass building on Madison? That's hers too. Yonkers girl. Bag. Secured. From what I read, Madison was on her way to securing some account that would have netted her over 500 million in her pocket, which means the business was going to make a cool billion. But now she is in the morgue.

She wasn't a walk in the park either. She wasn't nice and sweet. You can't be nice and sweet and make it in the arenas in which she was playing. She was cutthroat, and she was nasty. She did what she needed to do to get where she needed to be, and sometimes that meant stepping on anybody in her way.

That's something we need to think about: If someone tried to ruin her before because of jealousy and envy, what made this person take the next step? Why would someone take her life?

I am telling you all of this so you know the scope of what you are dealing with. This isn't a regular whodunit. This was a calculated attack on a woman, a mogul, a powerhouse.

We have the four people who knew her best, sitting in interrogation rooms right now, waiting to talk to us. There are some things you need to know:

1. *Shut up—I will do all the talking. Crooks can smell a newbie from a mile away, and I don't have time for you to fuck this up. You will be monitoring the interrogation from behind the two-way glass. Our sound system is broken, so there will be a monitor set up; you can read the conversation as it is happening.*

2. *Pay attention—Just listen. Pay attention to what these people are telling us. Listen to the stories, listen to the comments, but don't listen to the emotion. Emotion is subjective and deceiving.*

3. *Everybody is a suspect—Do not allow relationships to cloud your judgment. Mothers kill their own kids. You picking up what I'm putting down?*

4. *You make the decision—We will talk to all four of them, and if you think we need to go back and hear more of someone's story, you tell me that. You choose the direction this case will go in, and that is the most important part of this entire investigation. If you choose wrong, we have to start from the beginning... SO STAY SHARP.*

Now that we have that out of the way, let the investigation begin. I trust, by the end of this, we will have it solved. I believe in you, Detective—well, Rookie—until proven otherwise.

INTERROGATION ROOM 1
MIRANDA MCGHEE: THE SISTER

"Ms. McGhee?"

"My name is Mrs. Williams-McGhee."

"Okay...Mrs. Williams-McGhee, how are you holding up?"

"How do you think I'm holding up? Somebody just murdered my sister! My only sister! I'm fucked up, Detective, but how are you this morning?"

"Understood."

"Do you really understand?"

"Probably not, but what can you do to help me understand?"

"Kill your sister! Leave her in the street shamelessly and then call everybody she knew and have them come see her like that."

"Miranda—"

"I'm sorry."

"I'll be honest with you; I have no idea the pain you must feel right now. On top of the loss of your sister, you received a call and had to go to a crime scene and see her like that. I wouldn't wish that on anyone. At all. Your reaction is understandable, even if I cannot relate to your pain."

Miranda begins crying.

"Miranda, in order for me to do my job effectively, I need to know everything about your sister."

"She was a bitch. She was born that way."

"Talk to me about growing up with her."

"Life without her was amazing. I was my parents' first child, and because of that, I was able to get something from them she never could."

"And what is that?"

"Honesty."

"Care to elaborate?"

"No."

"Continue."

"I am four years older than my sister. Well, I *was* four years older than my sister. There were perks that came with being older than her that have lasted our entire lives. But there are some pretty shitty things that came with being her sister as well."

"Care to elaborate about that?"

"Sure."

"Continue."

"Around age thirteen, they realized that Maddy was supersmart. Genius, savant, you know—those kinds of nouns began being used to describe her. I was seventeen. I had been smart the entire time. No one used those words to describe me. She played basketball, volleyball, and ran track. People called her athletic, competitive, great, shit like that. I played varsity basketball all four years of high school. You know what they said about me?"

"What?"

"There is Miranda McGhee, Maddy McGhee's sister. Wonder where Maddy learned to play so well."

"Damn."

"Yeah. I never understood that; I came first, but I was compared to someone so much younger. So then I tried harder to stand out. I needed to be Miranda McGhee, the oldest of the McGhee sisters. Typically, when you are the oldest, you are revered, respected, regarded. Birth order gives you a space no one can take from you because, no matter what, you came first. That was not my experience. I was compared to someone who was developmentally below me in every way, and I could never escape."

"How was that for you?"

"Are you listening to me?"

"Yes, I am."

"Did you just hear what I said? My little sister is treated like the big sister...she *was*. I am going to have to start getting used to saying *was*. I am back to being the only sister. I spend four years the only sister...and thirty-five sharing—full circle, I guess."

"That is an interesting conclusion to draw."

"Is it?"

"It is."

"How?"

"Miranda, I am not trying to make anything difficult for you. As a matter of fact, I want to make it my sole priority to make sure you and your family find justice for this loss. I need you to find solace in this moment. You do not have to be combative with me."

"With all due respect, Detective, you having me sit in a room in the police station after seeing my sister butchered in the middle of the street goes against everything you just said you are trying to do for me and my family."

"I just want a full understanding of who Maddy was."

"You don't know her! You can't call her that!"

"My apologies, Madison."

Madison cries again.

"Miranda, I need you to help me with this. Tell me who Madison was so I can do my part."

"She was everything I wasn't, and everybody knew it."

"What makes you say that?"

"Everything between us has been a competition since she was able to spell the word. Even down to our looks. I was allowed to start wearing makeup at sixteen, which made my sister twelve at the time. We would go out and people would look at me and say, 'Miranda, I see you are trying to keep up with Madison's natural beauty.' Maddy took that and ran with it. Everywhere we went, everything she did, and how she looked had to be presented in a way that made her stellar and me the wannabe."

"You are both very beautiful, so I don't understand."

"Beauty is in the eye of the beholder, Detective, and to everyone who looked at us, while we may look just alike, she was the pretty sister. She was the pretty sister, the smart sister, the outgoing sister, the sister who would make it."

"And what did that make you?"

"What's the opposite of pretty?"

"Ugly."

"What's the opposite of smart?"

"Stupid, dumb."

"What's the opposite of outgoing?"

"Introverted."

"And what is the opposite of someone who would make it?"

"Someone who would fail."

"Very good, Detective, you figured out what it made me."

"And how did that make you feel?"

"I hate her."

"Madison?"

"Yes."

"Are you saying you hate her like 'I hate you, but I really love you; you just get on my nerves right now,' or do you hate her like 'I need to check your alibi'?"

"Do I look like I murdered my sister, Detective Shank?"

"I cannot investigate based on looks."

"Are you done insulting me?"

"You said it."

"I meant it. You asked me how it made me feel. I hated her for even existing because, once she existed, I no longer had an identity. That doesn't mean that I wanted her dead. I love my sister. Do I feel I have been functioning in her shadow her entire life? Absolutely, I do, and I have the right to feel that way because it is true! I had to fight for everything...just to be seen! I had to be bigger than, and better than...not because it was an achievable measurement, but just to be on the same damn playing fields with the incomparable Madison. How do you think I felt? Less than, small, and unseen."

"With that said, did you ever feel like your life would be better if Madison didn't exist?"

"Of course, I did."

"So..."

"So what? That wasn't an option. She does exist; she *did* exist. Life had to be altered to the fact that she did exist."

"Let me ask you this. So what in your life did you have that was separate from your sister? What do you do for a living?"

"I am an attorney at McGhee and Associates."

"Your sister's firm."

"Yes."

"Did you receive your JD before or after Madison?"

"After."

"How?"

"Great question. How did the older sister manage to finish school after the younger sister? Madsion went to NYU at sixteen; I had already been there for two years. Madison finished undergrad by nineteen and then entered law school. I was twenty-four, finishing up undergrad after taking a year off, and then I went to law school. She graduated at twenty-three. I was thirty when I finished my JD and passed the bar."

"Why did you take a year off?"

"Mental exhaustion brought on by a mental breakdown."

"Care to elaborate?"

"No."

"Why did it take you seven years to finish law school?"

"Same reason."

"So it is safe to say you have mental-health issues?"

"Wouldn't you have mental-health issues if all your life you were told you weren't good enough?"

"This isn't about me; I am asking you."

"Yes."

"Do you have a diagnosis?"

"Yes."

"Do you mind telling me what that is?"

"Will that help you figure out who my sister is...*was*...and who killed her?"

"Maybe."

"Manic depression."

"What is that?"

"What the fuck, Detective! You asking this shit like psychology was your minor in school or something, and you really don't know shit!"

"All symptoms and reason for diagnosis are different, Miranda. I just don't want to assume."

"My manic episodes sometimes have high energy, reduced need for sleep, and loss of touch with reality. On the other hand, my depressive episodes may show up as low motivation and loss of interest in daily activities. And then I want to kill myself."

"So you're suicidal."

"If I just said, 'And then I want to kill myself,' what does that mean, Detective."

"I want to be clear."

"Yes, I can be suicidal...*not* homicidal."

"Death is death, right?"

"Do you have to take sensitivity training to be in your position? Because, if so, you failed...bad."

"I am not being insensitive, Miranda, I am just asking questions."

"You are acting like you think I did it, so just ask me point-blank what it is you want to know."

"I'd rather let you keep talking, and if there is something else that stands out, I will do just that."

"What else do you want me to say."

"I want to know about Madison's private life."

"She wasn't even gay until I decided to be gay!"

"Huh?"

"My sister dated men until she was eighteen."

"Explain this to me. From what I assumed, with both of you being lesbians, I thought I could prove the fact that homosexuality is something that is in your DNA, but you are saying it was a choice for her."

"Number one, assuming makes an ass out of you and me, so let's be careful because I can be an ass by myself. Number two, I do not know if Madison had always been naturally attracted to men or not.

"What I do know is that when I was in college, I began exploring my attraction to women. I met a woman who was from Philly. Brittany Collier. Fine as hell. After her, there was no more exploring; it was a thing. I was a lesbian, and if she was the type of woman that I could have, I was going to go ahead and turn my straight card in. It was the summer of my junior year, and reality is, Madison and I had nothing to do with each other on campus, so she had no idea what I was doing.

"Anyways, I come home for the Fourth of July barbecue, and I have Brittany with me. My family lost their shit!"

"Not supportive?"

"Not in the least bit. It was so embarrassing. Maddy was one of the main ones asking what I was thinking, and telling me that our parents hadn't raised us that way. My mother was sick to her stomach. Like, literally, she threw up. Needless to say, Brittany did not want to deal with my family's foolishness. Fast-forward to Labor Day of that same year, I show up at the family barbecue, and who is sitting there, holding hands with a woman?"

"Madison?"

"Damn right, Madison."

"How?"

"I wondered the same shit."

"My family was smiling and congratulating her, telling her how proud they were that she was brave enough to come out. And then they had the nerve to look at me and say, 'Miranda, Maddy found a woman of caliber.'"

"Wasn't Brittany a premed student?"

"Mm-hmm. That wasn't good enough. Madison went to Mount Sinai and got an actual lesbian doctor and brought her home."

"That's wild."

"That's my life."

"So your family accepted her and her sexuality. When did they accept you and yours?"

"Did they ever?"

"Aren't you married to a woman?"

"Craziest thing, right?"

"Let me get this straight—"

"There is nothing straight about either of us, Detective"—clears her throat—"just my observation of you and why you are observing me."

"Your family took everything you did and made it bad, wrong, or an issue, but Madison could do the exact same thing and be praised."

"Bingo."

"Are you still close to your family?"

"Depends on how this will play out."

"What do you mean?"

"If you don't find the killer, Detective, I won't have a family anymore because they will be convinced that I took their golden child from them. So my suggestion would be, if you are truly concerned about our family, stop me from losing everybody at once." Miranda begins crying.

INTERROGATION ROOM 2
AUBREY WILLIAMS-MCGHEE: THE SISTER-IN-LAW

"Good morning, Mrs. Williams-McGhee."

"You can just call me Aubrey."

"Aubrey."

"Good morning, Detective."

"I apologize for the wait. How are you holding up?"

"It's kinda surreal, you know?"

"This kind of thing usually is."

"Until today, I had never seen a murdered, bloody body before."

"Most people are fortunate enough to go their entire lives and never have to see someone they love in that state."

"Yeah."

"I want to ask you some questions if you don't mind."

"Sure, anything."

"Let's start from the beginning. How did you get introduced to the McGhee family?"

"Wow, it's been over ten years now. I met Miranda randomly in FAO Schwarz. She was working there while she was finishing up her law degree, and I was in there because I am a big kid; I wanted to see what they had for the holidays."

"Sounds cute."

"It wasn't. She was really mean to me."

"I believe it."

"I see you've met my wife."

Shared laughter.

"I had actually gone up to Miranda to ask for help. There was a section of mini things like mini Slinky, mini Rubik's Cube, and mini Monopoly game. I wanted to know if there was a mini Clue game, and she looked at me and said 'Do you see a mini Clue game?' I looked around and said to her 'If I saw one, would I be asking for your help?' And it was like magic; we fell in love."

"Still cute."

"Slightly cute, because that right there was a tough cookie to crack. Did she tell you about her mental-health battles?"

"Reluctantly."

"I'm sure. Miranda and I took a while to begin dating. Part of it was because she was battling if she wanted to try with a woman again."

"Was she dating men?"

"I honestly do not know. I believe not; she just wasn't dating at all, but I am not entirely sure about that."

"Interesting."

"It took about eight or nine months for us to go on our first date, and that sent her into a depression. Being with me triggered her and brought back memories of her family and her first girlfriend."

"Brittany Collier."

"Oh wow, Miranda told you everything, I see."

"Probably not, but she told me enough."

"Do you want to continue to hear about our initial love story, or you want me to move on to when I first met Madison?"

"Are you the detective, or am I?"

"Military police for five years."

"Interesting again."

"Very."

"Let's move on to Madison."

"Miranda had been preparing me to meet Maddy for months before I actually met her. She told me her sister was nasty and mean, and..."

"Just like her!"

"No, she was painting the worst version of her, so I was preparing to meet Evilline from *The Wiz*. We walked into the house, and I met Glenda."

"Glenda?"

"My first interaction with Madison, she was charming and funny. She was warm and embracing; it was a totally different person than whom Miranda had been describing. I honestly looked at Miranda like, 'Are you lying to me? What is really going on here?'"

"How did Miranda react to Madison?"

"She spazzed out! She went crazy! She accused Maddy of being fake and trying to take my attention from her, and trying to present as a better person than she was."

"Did you think Madison was doing that?"

"At the time, no."

"Care to elaborate?"

"Sure. In that moment, Maddy presented as a little sister who was happy for the older sister that she adored. She gawked at Miranda and complimented her. She couldn't keep her hands off her hair or stop asking about her clothes; she seemed to be completely in love with her sister. I saw nothing wrong with it. My little sister be all over me. It seemed like a normal big-sister, littler-sister thing, but Miranda was not into it. Their mom was on Miranda for being so mean to Maddy, and then she just exploded, but that made Maddy look innocent because Miranda was so unhinged."

"I don't understand what you mean when you say 'look innocent.' Was she not?"

"Not by any definition of the word."

"Okay."

"That is one thing about Maddy. That girl is about a life that is circulated with manipulation and gaslighting. She is a pro at the shit she does, and if you are not careful, you will fall right into the trap."

"Sounds like you fell into the trap."

"At first, I didn't."

"How is that possible?"

"Easy, you can't fall into something you don't believe in."

"Seems like, to me, that's the trap itself."

"You would think, but not with Madison McGhee. You got to see the trap in front of you before you fall into it, and that's what sets her aside from anyone else I've ever met."

"So you feel Madison was genuine in that moment?"

"I didn't say that."

"But you just said—"

"What I said, I recognized the behavior based on my own experience with my family; the McGhees are not the Williamses."

"Who are the McGhees?"

"After all these years, I am still not sure that I know that answer."

"Interesting. Please continue."

"I will be honest; if you would have asked me that day I met Maddy if she would be someone I would have to eventually face off with, I would have told you no. Miranda is hands down the issue."

"Face off?"

"Yes, face off."

"Care to elaborate?"

"I'm sure we will get there sooner than later."

"Understood; continue."

"I honestly had a hard time trusting Miranda, for a while after that incident, because I couldn't believe the things she said because the action that was coming from her sister did not match anything she said, and this went on for years. We dated three years before we got married, and Maddy was nice to me the entire time. I know part of her condition causes her to alter reality, so I struggled hard with that. I struggled with even the idea of having a wife who was, from my position, delusional."

"You speak as if Miranda was right."

"I was raised to give everyone a chance. You do not take someone's word about someone else that you have never encountered. That is not only ignorant, but it just isn't fair. So it wasn't that Miranda was right or wrong, but I, Aubrey, needed to experience that behavior from Maddy myself before I treated her any kind of way."

"Did Miranda treat her any kind of way?"

"Absolutely."

"Meaning?"

"Miranda was a bitch!"

"Really?"

"Anytime we would be together and Maddy would call her, it would be 'What the fuck do you want? Why are you calling me? Don't you have someone else to ask?'"

"But doesn't Miranda work for Madison? Well, *didn't* she?" Silence. "Aubrey?"

"I'm sorry. You correcting yourself made this real again."

"I'm so sorry, Aubrey. I did notice that you continued to refer to her in the present tense. I know this is fresh and difficult. I won't do that again if that helps you."

"It doesn't, and it's not your fault."

"Please finish."

"Miranda works at the firm and was even offered co-ownership with Maddy."

"Miranda turned it down?"

"She felt like Maddy was trying to make a fool of her."

"How?"

"I didn't understand it then, and I don't understand it now. You will have to get it from her, and I am almost sure you will not understand it either."

"Noted."

"Up until our wedding, I saw Madison, Maddy, as a caring person who worked hard and got what she wanted."

"What changed at the wedding?"

"First of all, Miranda was adamant that Maddy had nothing to do with our wedding."

"Really?"

"Yes, and I was so very confused. I have four siblings, and I wanted each and every one of them to have something to do in our wedding—usher, best woman, best man, ring holder, something—but Miranda was like no. No family on either side. I felt that was so harsh and uncalled-for. I had not witnessed Maddy do anything to Miranda, so a week or so before the wedding, I called Maddy behind Miranda's back."

"Why would you do that?"

"What do you mean?"

"Your soon-to-be wife has expressed pure detest for this person and has blatantly stated that she does not want her to have anything to do with her day."

"Yes."

"So why would you call Maddy?"

"I wanted to know the truth."

"About?"

"Her relationship with Miranda."

"From Madison's perspective?"

"Exactly."

"Understood. Continue."

"I called Maddy, and she was her usual sweet self. I said to her, 'Maddy, I need to ask you something, and I need you to be honest.' And she said, 'I don't know any other way to be.' Then I said, 'Why does Miranda think you are the devil?' And she started laughing hysterically. So hysterical I started thinking maybe both of they asses is bipolar. After a while, she finally calmed down and said, 'My sister has been mad since the day I was born, and she will be mad until the day I die.'"

"That's cryptic."

"Very."

"And you said?"

"I didn't say anything immediately. Eventually, I said, 'What have you done to assist in her thoughts about you?' and she said very confidently, 'I have been myself, which unfortunately is better than her.'"

"Damn."

"Right."

"Okay, so the point of this conversation was what?"

"I no longer had one."

"Okay."

"When the wedding came, everything was beautiful. Our families were there, and the day went off without a hitch...until the reception, when my wife got drunk."

"It was her reception; she had the right."

"She absolutely did. What she did not have the right to do was try to put Maddy out of the reception."

"Why did she try to put her out?"

"She said that Maddy was only there to show her up and dress better than her."

"Was this true?"

"Did Maddy look beautiful? Absolutely, she did, but she looks like that without trying. I highly doubt she woke up that morning and said to herself, 'Self, let's make me immaculately beautiful today at my sister's wedding so she can look like the ugly duckling and everyone will look at me.' You can't make me believe, to this day, that was done on purpose."

"So what happened?"

"Miranda started throwing things and acting crazy and cussing and shit, and her mother was so embarrassed. So I caught myself stepping in and fixing it, and for the first time, I faced off with Maddy."

"Weren't you defending Maddy?"

"It's not that kind of face-off, Detective."

"I'm not sure I understand. What you mean?"

"I mean Miranda was the one who got kicked out, and that left me there with Maddy in the reception."

"That doesn't sound right at all."

"In hindsight, it wasn't. I played right into the idea that Miranda was the issue. Was she a problem? Yes, nothing about what she did made sense, but I should have left with my wife. When her family made it okay to remove her and continue the reception, I was content with that."

"So how did you face off with Madison?"

"Toward the end of the night, as things were winding down, Maddy asked me if I wanted to dance."

"Harmless enough."

"For now."

"Okay…"

"While we were dancing, she laid her head on my chest and started crying. When I asked her why, she said, 'My sister hates me, and there is nothing I can do about it.' That broke my heart because, for me, it solidified my thoughts that Maddy wasn't who Miranda thought she was, and it started me on my journey of defending and standing up to Miranda on Maddy's behalf."

"What about the face-off that you were talking about? This isn't seeming as if it is turning into a combative thing."

"Detective, all face-offs are not combative. The concept of a face-off is two competitors getting into the ring, onto the field, on the court, preparing for a one-on-one competition."

"Okay…"

"Remember that trap I told you about, the one you had to see coming before you fell into it?"

"Yes."

"Game on."

INTERROGATION ROOM 3
DR. DIMITRIA KINCAID: THE THERAPIST

"Dr. Kincaid, I apologize for the wait, but I appreciate your patience."

"No worries."

"I am not sure how much we can discuss here; I am fully aware of patient confidentiality."

"I will answer what I can, and what I can't, I won't."

"Fair enough. How long have you been treating Madison?"

"I began having sessions with Madison about ten years ago."

"So you know her just as well as anyone else?"

"Yes, if not better."

"I was just about to say that."

"Yes."

"How are you doing with all of this?"

"If I am honest, I am used to losing patients, usually to suicide. This was different, but still the same end result. I am not okay, but I will be."

"You are very poised."

"Thank you."

"What is your background?"

"Undergraduate degree from Winston-Salem State University. Master's degree from North Carolina A & T State University. Second master's degree from Regent University. Doctorate from Columbia University."

"Wow. That is impressive."

"Thank you."

"Two HBCUs, Christian school, and Ivy League."

"I see you are well-versed in the academic realm."

"Something like that. It just comes with the territory."

"I'm sure."

"May I ask you something off topic?"

"If you must."

"Why the Christian school?"

"In order for me to be a well-rounded doctor, I needed a well-rounded education. I got the same master's twice, with two different experiences. It made me better at my job."

"Understood."

"About Madison."

"Yes, about Madison. Can you tell me some of the things she was dealing with?"

"Madison was about twenty-four when we had our first session; she had just finished law school and was slightly lost in the world."

"How? She graduated law school at the age of twenty-three. How can someone so successful be so lost?"

"That's exactly how it happens. The amount of pressure put on Madison to be that successful pushed her to lose herself."

"What do you mean?"

"I am unsure the amount of education needed to have your position. Can you enlighten me?"

"I have an associate's in criminal justice."

"So it is safe to say that your job is based on experience and not education?"

"I have training and things of that nature that helped me climb the ranks."

"So it is safe to say that your job is based on experience and not education?"

"Yes."

"In that type of work, your performance is your pressure. You have to make sure that you are executing excellently to make it to the next level. Correct?"

"Correct."

"Imagine that, and then add the pressure of age—young age— familial expectation, and the rigorous schedule of school. All at the same time."

"I never thought of it like that."

"And most don't."

"So where was she mentally?"

"She wasn't."

"Okay."

"Madison had a troubled childhood."

"Really?"

"I'm sure you spoke to her sister, correct?"

"Correct."

"Did she tell you about their father?"

"Actually, no one has mentioned the father during any of this."

"Humph."

"And that means what?"

"If I can be candid...?"

"Sure."

"He fucked those kids up."

"Please explain that."

"The rivalry between Madison and Miranda came from their father, David. David McGhee. I am sure you will have some good reading material if you reach out to the Yonkers Police Department."

"Why do you say that?"

"What do you know about this family?"

"Obviously, not a damn thing."

"Are you from the area?"

"No."

"Where are you from, Detective?"

"Buffalo."

"Oh, so you are not a real New Yorker?"

"That's how they tend to describe us, but Buffalo is New York."

"Melinda McGhee killed David McGhee when Madison was fifteen and Miranda was turning twenty."

"What? Why? Why isn't she in prison?"

"They don't put people in prison for self-defense, Detective Shank."

Silence.

"David McGhee had been molesting Miranda and beating Madison for their entire lives. Melinda knew nothing about it. Miranda was always upset because what was happening to her was much more horrific than what was happening to Madison. Madison would get beat to be better, so then Madison, being the smarter of the two, would exceed all expectations so she could spare herself the pain that came with her father's wrath. Miranda, on the other hand, took it in silence."

"And their mom didn't know?"

"All she knew was the knocks upside the head she was receiving her damn self, so her antennas weren't where they needed to be to fix that."

"Wow. So what made her kill him?"

"She walked in on him getting ready to rape Miranda. Up until that point, he had only touched her, but she was showing signs of being gay, and David was not for that. David told her he had been preparing her for men, so her opposition to men was infuriating to him. When Melinda attempted to save Miranda, he knocked her out cold, unconscious.

"Madison came in from basketball practice to find her mother on the floor, bleeding from her head, and her sister bent over the couch. Madison threw the ball at David and rushed to Miranda's side. Enraged, David—pants down, dick still swinging—threw Madison down and attempted to climb on top of her and show her who was running that house.

"In the midst of all of this, Melinda regained consciousness. She saw what was happening, and she stabbed him."

"How many times?"

"The coroner's report said he was stabbed twenty-seven times."

"And both girls saw this?"

"Yes."

"Damn."

"Damn is right."

"What effect did this have on Madison?"

"It made her even more of an overachiever because she survived. Miranda didn't survive; mentally, she died that day because she was physically violated in such an unimaginable way. Madison had to sort through that."

"And you helped her with that?"

"To a degree."

"Meaning?"

"I mean, will she ever get over having a physically abusive father, and walking in on him raping her sister, her mother unconscious on the floor, her attempted rape from her father, and then witnessing her mother take his life?"

"I guess not."

"I think not."

"So can I ask you about Miranda?"

"I never treated Miranda; anything I tell you about her will be hearsay."

"Isn't it all hearsay at this point?"

"Everything I just told you is public record."

"Okay...Madison."

"Yes?"

"How was her recovery from that?"

"She threw herself into success, but then she achieved the highest point she could at that moment. A bar-card-holding attorney at twenty-three years old, and she realized she didn't know what love was; all she knew was she had a desire for something she had never experienced."

"But she had had a girlfriend by this point; we know that."

"So."

"So?"

"What does that mean?"

"How had she not experienced love?"

"Did you love every man—or woman, I don't know your life—you ever dealt with?"

"No."

"Then why would you assume she did?"

"Understood."

"From Madison's perspective, the only love that was pure came from her mother, the murderer. Her sister hated her, and her father hurt her. She became cold in how she operated; that's what that environment created."

"So she wasn't sweet?"

"No, there is no sweet in that. She was human, and she had feelings, and she was able to create bonds, but she was flawed because mentally she was broken."

"And you helped her sort through that?"

"Enough."

"And that means...?"

"I helped create the monster known as Madison McGhee."

"Monster."

"Yes."

"So you are leaning in Miranda's direction in this."

"No."

"No?"

"No. I have already told you I cannot speak on Miranda; I can only speak on my interactions with Madison."

"What made her a monster?"

"Once she learned her own power—something that had been hidden inside of her—she used it for evil, not good."

"What does that mean?"

"If she were on Wall Street, she would be considered the Wolf of Wall Street. Madison's grit and grind came with her stepping on everybody's head and neck, no matter the cost. She didn't get those buildings because she's caring and compassionate. There is no compassion in being a shark in the business world. Sharks can have 35,000 to 50,000 teeth throughout the course of their lives. Madison had 100,000."

"So you are telling me anybody could want to kill her."

"Absolutely."

"That doesn't help."

"I'm sorry, Detective; I'm not here to do your job for you."

"Okay."

"Madison wasn't somebody well-liked."

"What do you know about her sexual-assault case?"

"It was bullshit."

"I figured."

"That was a case conjured up by Angel Bellamy, a former attorney at her firm."

"Angel Bellamy."

"Again, public record."

"I will make sure we investigate Angel."

"Angel isn't a murderer. Angel was a jilted sex toy that felt that if she slept with the boss, she would make her way to the top."

"So they did sleep together?"

"Absolutely, but Madison was no fool. Angel approached Madison. She pursued Madison. She seduced Madison. Madison made it clear, if they slept together, Angel would have to leave the firm, but when Madison asked for her resignation, Angel lost her mind and accused Madison of rape, triggering Madison's memories of her father."

"The case went away."

"Because genius Madison had video, audio, and paper trails of the escalation of the relationship and made dumbass Angel sign an NDA that included the resignation that she was later asked for."

"Madison was smart."

"Somewhat."

"You like to challenge the conclusions I come to."

"I like accuracy in the summarization that you make of my statements."

"So what does *somewhat* mean in this instance?"

"Smart would have been to never deal with Angel and put everything Madison had ever worked for in danger. I do not celebrate her for keeping the paper and digital trail; the whole thing should have never happened."

"Understood."

"Humph."

"Let me ask you this—"

"Okay."

"Would you consider Madison a friend?"

"I used to."

"Okay. Did Madison trust you?"

"More than anybody in her life."

"So is it safe to say you were the healthiest relationship she had until she died?"

"Somewhat."

INTERROGATION ROOM 4
TEN BROADWAY: THE ASSISTANT

"Mr. Broadway?"

"If y'all don't let me up out of here, I'ma kill somebody!"

"I'm unsure if that's something you should say in the middle of a murder investigation."

"You right. I take it back."

"You can't take it back."

"Too late. I already did. Next!"

"Okay, well, I'm sure you know why you're here."

"Because somebody done killed Madison. Lawd! Why her, Jesus?"

"Mr. Broadway?"

"Yes?"

"You can stop the stunts and show; they don't move me."

"Ain't nobody trying to move you, girl! I am in mourning. Can't you tell?"

"I can tell you're dramatic."

"Shade."

"Let me know when you are done."

"I will. Lawwwwwwwwwwwwwwwwd, why Madison? Why her, Jesus? She didn't deserve that, Lawwwwwwwwwwwwwd. Take me instead, Jesus! Bring me home, LAWDDDDDDDDD. I can't be here without her, JESUSSSSSSSSSS! I'm done now."

"Thank you."

"You're welcome."

"Is Ten your real name?"

"Is Detective yours?"

Silence.

"My name is TrenTen Aloysius Broadway, and I'm a Cancer."

"Which means Ten is a part of your name."

"That, it is."

"Okay."

"Okay."

"Are you ready to discuss Madison now?"

"Lawwwwwwwwwwwwwwwwd, don't know if I can take this, Jesus! She just out there, lying in the street, just dead. She's just dead."

"Yes, but that's not what I want to discuss."

"Oh, what you want to talk about, girl?"

"Madison—"

"Lawwwwwwwdddd—"

"Stop it."

Silence.

"I need you to get a grip."

"Grip gotten."

"Tell me about your relationship with Madison."

"I was her assistant until about six months ago."

"What happened?"

"I'd rather not discuss that."

"Okay. How long were you her assistant?"

"Three wonderful years."

"Wonderful?"

"I said wonderful, didn't I?"

"What was wonderful about it?"

"I worked in a beautiful building, with beautiful people, and we came up with beautiful ideas to help other beautiful people advertise their work."

"So you worked at the advertising company."

"Yeah, girl, after that bitch played with Maddy at the law firm, she didn't fuck with them no more, chil'."

"But it was her firm."

"Ain't you a boss?"

"Yes."

"Do you got to work every day?"

"Yes."

"Then, girl, you ain't no real boss! Maddy owned the company and the damn building; she ain't have to deal with them folk in there! Plus, her sister was there; the show was going on. She was at the agency."

"Where she went to work every day?"

"Nope, bosses don't do that! I just told you."

"Then how did you assist somebody who was never there? Make this make sense!"

"Phones work. Email works. We do digital work; why she got to come to her office that's bein' ran by yours truly to do her work?"

"But you got fired."

"That was the other day. I was there for three years."

"How did you run the office if you weren't the office manager?"

"'Cause she told me to!"

"Did you always do everything she told you to?"

"Yup."

"Then why did you get fired?"

"I'd rather not discuss that."

"You are trying me."

"Am I?"

"Tell me about the advertising world."

"Dog eat dog, chil'. Ain't nothing nice about it."

"Didn't you just call everybody beautiful?"

"In the face, girl! Whole office, every client—just gorgeous. I mean, look at me; I am a representation."

"But you got fired."

"Bring it up again!"

"Continue."

"As I was saying, it is tough being in advertising. People steal; people lie; people are treacherous; they just ain't shit. And that is every day, all day. It is a big-ass competition to get the biggest clients and create the best ads to make sure your client makes money so they keep coming back to you."

"This makes it safe to say there are no friends in advertising?"

"No, girl, ain't no friends. You can't be friends, ain't go'n' be around long enough to be friends with no damn body. If you ain't creative and innovative, you ain't in the firm. Period!"

"Did you consider Madison your friend?"

"Did you just hear what I said?"

"But you were there three years, working side by side with her."

"We were friendly; I will say that. She knew a lot of my business, but I didn't know nothing about her. I do know at one point she was talking to two women, and right around when I was released from my duties—"

"Fired."

"Shade! Anyways, things went south with both of them, but I don't know the tea on that, chil'."

"Names?"

"Nope."

"Nicknames?"

"Nope."

"Terms of endearment?"

"Baby."

"No help."

"I don't know why you asked me after I told you I did not know in the first damn place. Woooo saaaaa. Rub them ears, honey, like Martin did on *Bad Boys 2*. WOOOOOO SAAAAAAAAAA."

"Ten, I'ma arrest you."

"For what?"

"Because I been up all damn night, and you are playing in my damn face."

"I'm sorry, girl. What you want to know?"

"About Madison."

"BIGGEST BITCH IN THE WORLD."

"Now we are getting somewhere."

"Where we getting?"

"To Madison."

"Dead."

"So she's a dead bitch."

"Oh, you disrespectful!"

"You said it."

"You right; I did. She *was* a bitch though. Girlfriend did not play, okay? She ran a tight ship."

"Explain that a little more for me, if you will."

"Of course, girl. Pride Ads is a new agency, compared to other agencies in New York, and Madison is used to being on the top. So she ran the agency as if she were the number one firm in the damn world. There were no games played when it came to her. At all. If your ad was trash and got rejected, you were out the door. The big clients she took on herself. I never really understood where she got the knowledge because she is a lawyer. So who the hell taught her to be in advertising? But she was knocking shit out the park. It went from a start-up to a real contender in three years. She worked her ass off."

"I don't see where the bitch comes in."

"It comes in because she didn't give two fucks who she hurt while she was making Pride Ads a name in New York. Mama, daddy, sister, brother, cousin—anybody can get it."

"Her father is dead."

"Lawwwwwwwwwwwwwwwwwd! Not another dead McGhee, Jesus! Pray for that family!"

"Ten..."

"Yes?"

"He's been dead a long time."

"Oh, then, chil', just pray for me."

"Your story..."

"Yes?"

"Finish it."

"Gotcha."

"Now."

"Honestly, Madison was cool until she wasn't. You know what I mean? Like, when I say we were friendly, I mean that. We laughed, we talked, we ate, we spent time together, and at no point did

I ever feel like those moments weren't genuine. But when she had to get on somebody's ass, or when her name was on the line, or her reputation was in jeopardy, that switch would get switched, and, babyyyy, she had a PhD in bitchology!"

"Give me an example."

"Picture it—Sicily, 1925—"

"Jail."

"Okay, I'm for real. I think I was working there about thirty to thirty-five days, give or take a few weekends and a few days off, 'cause, girl, you know I had a man then, and we had things to do."

"Ten..."

"Okay. A inquiry came in from Trump Towers, and the entire office was like, 'Uh-uh, girl, we ain't about to give that nigga no money!'"

"Nigga?"

"He act like one."

"Wow."

"I know I'm a trip. Pray for me."

"Finish the story."

"Right. So, anyways, Madison called a meeting with the best team of designers in the company, and she was like, 'Check this out; I am about my money. I don't give a fuck who he is. I did my research, and his name is the only thing about him attached to the Trump Towers; he is not affiliated. This means all the ruckus that you are causing about this is a moot point for me. You have two options—do it or quit. You have two minutes to make your decision.' Babyyy, them people got to talking back to Ms. Madison, and, baby, she fired all them muthafuckas on the spot! I ain't never seen nothing like it. Took that shit, and got the client on her own, and that's how she made her first million with Pride Ads."

"I still don't hear the bitch in what happened."

"She ruined like twenty lives!"

"They had a job to do and wouldn't do it. She gave them options; they pushed back. Sounds like they fired themselves."

"Cold-blooded."

"Who?"

"You."

"How?"

"You don't care about them people's lives; they had bills."

"Everybody's got bills!"

"That's true."

"As a boss, I understand fully she did what she needed to do to ensure her business stayed afloat, and those people were in the way of that."

"Did you know Maddy?"

"No."

"Girl, you sound just like her."

"Look at that, and I go to work every day."

"That's right; you ain't nothing like her."

"Did anything happen with those people?"

"I think they tried to sue her, but she's a lawyer, so she was already two steps ahead of them."

"How so?"

"I mean, you already said it. She didn't just fire them. She gave options, she laid out expectations, and they were not met. They were all contracted workers."

"Can you explain that to me?"

"Are you slow?"

"A little bit."

"The contracted people was like on contracts, you know. They weren't like regular office staff. They had to meet certain criteria in their contracts to keep their jobs. When they protested, there was a clause in the contracts that said that political affiliation and stuff couldn't come between them and work...because it was just work. When they made a stink—and it was a stink about the name Trump—it was over. They could have conceded, but they didn't, and Ms. Madison won that thang."

"Were you contracted?"

"No, ma'am."

"Hourly?"

"Shade."

"Were you?"

"Salary, thank you."

"Then can you answer this for me?"

"What is it, girl? I'm ready to go."

"Why did you get fired?"

"I'd rather not discuss that."

INTERROGATION ROOM 1
MIRANDA MCGHEE: THE SISTER

"Miranda, I'm sorry for the wait, but I appreciate you staying to continue this interview."

"Interview or interrogation?"

"You tell me."

"Are you ready to blatantly ask me if I killed my sister yet?"

"No, Id' rather you just talk to me."

"Okay."

"I have some follow-up questions that I want to sort through, if you don't mind."

"Okay."

"Tell me about your father."

"I don't have one."

"But you had one."

"David McGhee was never a father to me."

"What was he?"

"A sperm donor."

"Miranda, I know all of this is hard and a lot for you, but if you do not cooperate with me, I cannot help you bring justice for Madison."

"What does he have to do with anything?"

"He has everything to do with your relationship with your sister and how things got so bad. You were able to tell me all the things, but none of the things, because the bottom line is he started this relationship that you two have."

"Had." Begins crying.

"Miranda, please."

"Who told you about him?"

"It's public record."

"You didn't know before, so is that where you've been? Googling my family. Finding out I come from a rapist and a murderer. Great fucking genes, right? Guess my manic depression made sense to you once you read the articles and saw the pictures?"

"I did not do any of that."

"THEN WHO TOLD YOU?"

"Why is that so important to you?"

"Because whoever told you can go to hell for bringing this up right now when my sister is dead!" Cries harder.

"You didn't really hate Madison, did you?"

"Yes!"

"No, you didn't. You hated the fact she was spared from something you weren't."

Silence.

"I believe, Miranda, that you truly loved your sister, but your childhood forced you into a situation that altered your idea of love. You cannot hate someone you never loved. And I will take it one step further—you hated your father and projected that pain onto Madison because he was no longer there!"

"I hated her because of her!"

"Why?"

"She waited until it was too late to stop him."

"You two were children."

"The first lesson you learn as a child is the difference between right and wrong."

"But if that lesson is being taught by someone who is wrong, do you truly learn it?"

"I told you; she was born a bitch."

"How, Miranda?"

"I remember when my parents brought her home from the hospital. I was so excited to have a little sister. So happy. And when I reached for her, she started crying."

"That's what babies do."

"It's the way she looked at me."

"Miranda, please, let's be realistic. Give me real things that justify what you say about Madison. If your father—"

"I don't have a father."

"If David groomed her to be your nemesis, how do you blame her for that?"

"BECAUSE SHE WAS SUPPOSED TO LOVE ME!"

"Do you know for a fact that your sister did not love you?"

Silence.

"Tell me a happy memory you have with Madison."

"David's funeral."

"Tell me about that."

"I don't know how this assists you in finding my sister's killer."

"It doesn't, but it assists you in remembering better times."

Silence.

"Tell me about David's funeral."

"My mom was in jail. David's parents had taken care of all the arrangements, and they felt it necessary for my sister and I to be in the building at that moment. We did not agree. So they bought us clothes to match the theme of the funeral. Royal purple and gold. We sat in our home, with people who were essentially strangers, and prepared to head to the church. Madison had come up with the idea that we get in the limo first. She would sneak the limo driver twenty dollars, and when David's parents got out of the car, we would take off and miss the service because they couldn't find us."

"Did her plan work?"

"Kinda."

"What happened?"

Simple chuckle.

"So Maddy gave the man the money. Mind you, David's parents were a few feet away when she did this, and I think our grandfather saw her. We get in the limo, get to the church, and nobody gets out of the car. We are sitting there like, 'What the hell is going on,' and they are looking at us look at them. Finally, Maddy says, 'You are going to be late.' And they looked at her and said, 'So are you.'"

Uncontrollable laughter.

"The funeral director then opened the door for them and tried to usher them out of the car, but they looked at us and said, 'You go first; climb over us.' I looked over at Maddy because I did not know what to do in the least bit. She climbed over them and got out. I followed her. Before they could get out—because, you know, they were old—Maddy slammed the car door and took off running. I took off behind her because she was not even about to leave me there with them."

"How long did you run?"

"It felt like forever, but I think that we ended up like two miles down the road, at an old bodega."

"You never went to the funeral?"

"Absolutely not. Why would I go in there and pretend to be sad?"

"You weren't sad that your father—"

"I already told you."

"David was dead?"

"No."

"Are you sad that Madison is dead?"

"Detective Shank, I am frankly tired of you insinuating but not directly asking me if I murdered Madison. I am offended, and you are insulting my intelligence."

"You are the one who said you hated her."

"And do."

"Not *did*?"

"I do."

"Then if you did not kill her, there is more to the story that you are not telling me. You already kept the things about David from me. What else could you possibly be hiding?"

"I didn't know not wanting to tell you that my pervert father molested me was hiding something. This, in fact, has nothing to do with my sister's investigation. You haven't asked me shit to do with her investigation yet."

"What makes you believe that?"

"Why haven't we talked about the call I got?"

"There are other things that seem to be more interesting."

"To whom?"

"Me."

"Are you going to ask me about the phone call?"

"I understand that you are the attorney in the room, but in this capacity, I have control, Mrs. Williams-McGhee, so you can stop with the manipulation."

Silence.

"However, since you brought it up, tell me about the phone call you got last night."

"Manipulation at its finest, Detective Shank. I was up later than usual."

"Why?"

"Some things on my mind."

"Care to elaborate?"

"No."

"Continue."

"I had just checked on my babies—"

"You have children?"

"Yes."

"With Aubrey?"

"Yes."

"How old are they?"

"My daughter is five, and my son is three."

"They *are* babies. Poor things. Where are they now?"

"I will get to that if you allow me to finish my story."

"My apologies."

"As I was saying, I had just finished checking on my babies, and I headed to the kitchen to make myself some white-chocolate peppermint tea and turn on Netflix. The first time my phone rang, I thought it was Aubrey."

"Aubrey was not home?"

"No."

"Interesting."

"Is it? Anyways, I grabbed my phone, and I saw that it was an unknown number. I don't do those during business hours, so I damn sure wasn't about to answer that call in the middle of the night. I put my phone back on the couch and went back to my tea. A few moments went by, and the phone started ringing again. I was like, 'What the fuck?' It annoyed me. Who was blowing my phone up like this?"

"Blowing it up?"

"Yes."

"But you have only mentioned two phone calls."

"That was at first; in the span of about fifteen minutes, I got at least twenty calls."

"May I see your phone?"

"Sure."

"Wow."

"I have nothing to lie to you about, Detective."

"Continue your story."

"At about two thirty-five, I believe, I finally answered it with 'Who is this?' I was pissed at this point because what do you want at that ungodly hour? It took a moment, and just as I was about to hang up, this voice said, 'Miranda, Maddy is dead.' It was bone-chilling." Begins to cry.

"Do you know if it was a man or woman on the phone?"

"I couldn't tell, to be honest. I didn't say anything. I just held the phone. Then they said, 'You might want to get to the 700 block of 154th Street; you may be able to save her.' Then the phone went dead."

"Then what did you do?"

"I called Aubrey, but she didn't answer."

"Why wasn't Aubrey home?"

"I honestly thought she was with Maddy, so in this moment, we both do not know where she was."

"Huh."

"The next thing I did was call my mom. My mom lives down the street from us, so she was there in about five minutes. I told her I would call her when I knew something, and I left. While I was driving, I kept calling Maddy, begging her to pick up the phone, but the phone kept going to voicemail. When I pulled up, the police were there, and Aubrey was already there. I knew it was true; I knew she was dead." Cries harder.

"I am so sorry, Miranda."

"The killer is so diabolical. They called me. They called you. They called Aubrey. They called Ten. They called Dr. Kincaid. This was done on purpose. There is no coincidence on who was called there that night. You too."

"Me?"

"Yes. Did you know my sister?"

"No, I didn't."

"Then you need to figure out the part you played in this, Detective."

"I don't think I understand what you are saying."

"It is no mistake that you are the detective, or person, that was called last night. We were all sent there for a reason. The killer wanted us all to see the demise of my sister. They wanted us all to see what they had done to her. They wanted us all to see how much they hated her. They wanted all of us to remember how she left this earth—each and every one of us."

"Why?"

"That's for you to figure out, Detective, and the first thing you need to figure out is why they chose you."

"I am a homicide detective. That is no secret. I have been in the news, in newspapers; my name is known around the city. That's the truth. They could have simply called because of that."

"How often do you solve your cases?"

"More often than not."

"Then I would assume you have been chosen because they want you to solve this crime, because you are the one they know can do it."

"Why would you assume that? I'm sure you told me not to assume earlier."

"Maybe I did, but I assume that's why you are a part of this now."

"And why did they call you?"

"Ask me."

"Miranda, did you murder Madison?"

"No."

"Would you pass a polygraph?"

"Yes."

"I need to ask you something about what you said to me earlier."

"I said a lot earlier; we have been talking all morning."

"It was about Aubrey."

"What about her?"

"You said that you figured she wasn't home because she was with Madison."

"Yeah."

"Why did you think that?"

"Because, Detective, Madison was fucking my wife."

Rookie, what do you think? Do you think Miranda killed Madison? If you do, Skip ahead to page 107 and finish her interview. If you are certain that she has nothing to do with it, let's continue on to the next interview room.

AUBREY WILLIAMS-MCGHEE: THE SISTER-IN-LAW

"Aubrey, Aubrey, Aubrey."

"Uh-oh."

"Uh-oh is right. Your wife just told me everything."

"She can't tell you everything when she doesn't know everything."

"Is that right?"

"I'm positive on that one."

"She seems to know something."

"Like what?"

"That you were sleeping with Madison."

Silence.

"She must have got that right."

"She did."

"Were you going to tell me you were sleeping with the victim who happens to be your wife's sister?"

"I'm sure we would have gotten to it eventually."

"Eventually is here. Start from the beginning."

"Well, I already told you about the wedding."

"Yes, so it started then?"

"No, no, no. Not at all."

"Then when did it start?"

"I think the attraction was always there. Maddy treated me different than Miranda, you know? It was never hard to laugh with Maddy. Life wasn't always heavy with her. When Miranda was on one, and straight bugging, Maddy would always find a way to stop me from going down the rabbit hole with Miranda."

"What do you mean?"

"I remember this one time before we had the kids; Maddy had come over to the house to go over something with Miranda; I don't really remember what it was. Anyways, Miranda wasn't understanding what Maddy was saying, and you could see her getting more and more frustrated by the moment. Miranda ended up knocking over my desk—which had a lot of things on it from when I was in the military and the different countries I'd visited—and my glass Eiffel Tower broke. Miranda had already reached the point of no return, and I was about to go there with her because I did not understand what my stuff had to do with her issue. Why tear my shit up? When I went to address Miranda—and I will admit I was going to match her energy—Maddy stepped in front of me. She looked me dead in my eyes and said, 'It's not worth it, Aub.' I stopped in my tracks for many reasons."

"And what were those reasons?"

"The first reason was the way she said, 'Aub.' Nobody else in the world calls me that. Only Maddy. It causes an instant sense of calm because it makes me feel seen. The second thing was she looked me dead in my eyes. She stopped me in my tracks. No one else, not even my wife, could command my attention in such a way, and it wasn't in an aggressive way. It was one of those things where it was like, again, 'I see you, and I know this is not you.' Lastly, there was no fear in her eyes. She was not worried about Miranda and her tirade, and that let me know that I shouldn't be either.

"Was I hurt she broke something that meant so much to me? Yes, I was devastated, but it was a material thing, and my wife is mentally sick, so I needed to take that into consideration."

"Let me get this straight..."

"Okay..."

"You knew Miranda's mental diagnosis before you married her, right?"

"Yes."

"How had you handled it leading up to this point?"

"With all due respect, Detective, is this interview about my marriage to Miranda or what happened to Madison?"

"In this moment, both. Answer the question."

"I hadn't really handled it, if I am honest."

"What does that mean?"

"It means that I had never dealt with anyone who was mentally battling anything. Not in a romantic sense. So I probably didn't even really take it seriously the first couple of years. My stance was always like, 'Get a grip. Deal with life, and move on.'"

"You're just insensitive?"

"I wouldn't call it insensitive, but when you haven't dealt with something, and you do not know the gravity of what they are dealing with, your ignorance can look like insensitivity."

"Understood. So you wanted Madison."

"No."

"You felt like Madison was more put together?"

"She is."

"So you felt you got the wrong sister?"

"No."

"How did you and Madison begin having an affair if you keep saying no?"

"Let me be clear. I loved Madison early on, and not in the way that you are thinking. She's my sister-in-law. I loved her because I was supposed to, and my wife is so hard on her; I felt like she need an ally in all of this. Madison would flirt, but it was never anything I paid any attention to. It was like, 'That's just her. Smile, accept the compliment, and move on.' There was no reason for me to think anything different of what she was doing."

"Can I be honest, Aubrey?"

"Sure."

"I call bullshit!"

"About what?"

"You are telling me this fine-ass woman was flirting with you; your wife, or soon-to-be wife wasn't really giving you what you needed—"

"Is that what you got out of what I said?"

"Isn't that why people cheat?"

"Miranda is an excellent wife and amazing mother. Nothing about her illness prevented her from giving me what I needed in our relationship or marriage. Does her illness create a toxic environment? Absolutely, but that doesn't mean she wasn't giving me what I needed."

"Then why cheat?"

"I told you; once a trap was set by Maddy, not even God can prevent you from falling into it."

"Make it make sense."

"I'm trying to, but I've never had to say all of this out loud."

"You ain't saying shit now."

"I'm trying to put it in a way that doesn't make me look like some type of trifling creep."

"I doubt that is possible."

"I don't need to be judged, Detective."

"Aubrey, you cheated on your wife with her sister, whom she hates. Trifling creep is a nice way of putting what you are."

"Wow."

"So is that why you killed her?"

"What?"

"Is that why you killed Madison?"

"I would never hurt her, no matter how fucked up she is!"

"That's different."

"Huh?"

"You have been praising Madison this entire time, and now, all of a sudden, she's fucked up?"

"We all have some fucked-up ways about us, and I'm sure you do too."

"What is that supposed to mean?"

"Nothing."

"So what was so fucked up about Madison?"

"I'll get to that."

"You are wasting my time, Aubrey."

"You brought me here. Who is wasting whose time here?"

"Tell me about the affair; tell me about something Madison did to make herself so irresistible that you would become a piece of shit. Tell me something!"

"Madison was never really in a relationship. She always had someone around, waiting in the shadows, but never in a full-on relationship. I found that to be odd, misleading, and intriguing."

"Now, we are getting somewhere. Why?"

"You've seen her. Well, when you saw her, she wasn't at her best, clearly, but you've seen her. She was fucking beautiful. Her skin was the color of someone out of Africa. Damn, what's the name of that actress in that show on Prime Video. Beautiful. Um, um, you know who Deborah Ayorinde is?"

"Yeah, I actually do."

"She had her color. Rich dark chocolate. Dark-black, long, thick hair, and her body—she spent just as much time in the gym as she did working to build her empire. She was the epitome of what a woman should look like. You already know how successful she was. Her place in Manhattan—bomb! Penthouse with amazing views of the city, decorated like it is something out of a magazine. Driving a clean-ass Maserati, custom-made. Anybody in their right mind would want her."

"But she was single."

"Single as a dollar bill."

"Because she was a bitch?"

"Miranda told you that, didn't she?"

"Amongst others."

"She was single because that just fucking makes life easier these days."

"So you stepped in to fill the void."

"No."

"Okay."

"Right before my wife got pregnant with our daughter, we were planning a trip to Greece for our five-year wedding anniversary."

"Okay."

"Miranda and I had everything laid out. Trip paid for. Romantic massages on the water, beautiful villa we were going to be staying, a private chef. Excursions paid for and ready for us to dive into Greek culture in a way neither of us had ever experienced. Then, about a week or so before the trip, Miranda started spiraling."

"What do you mean?"

"We had already been in talks and preparing to get pregnant, and when we got back from our trip, she was going to start her first round of hormone therapy. So, that week before, I go into the office, and she's sitting there staring out of the window. I'm like, 'Babe, what's wrong?' She never looked at me; she kept staring out the window, and she said, 'What if I make the baby crazy?' I was confused, but she was speaking about the fact that her mental-health issues could be passed on."

"Damn."

"Right. That entire week, each day she got deeper and deeper into a depression. It was something she couldn't shake, and then, the day before we were supposed to leave, she lost her shit on me. She blamed me for putting her in a position to hurt a child that didn't ask to be here. She told me I was a woman too; I could carry our child, but I chose to make her the villain. I was so confused. We had talked about it; we were both on board for it, and she wanted it. How did that make it my fault?

"When I woke up the next morning, she was gone. Her luggage was gone. I tried calling; I got nothing. I went looking for her before we needed to be at the airport; I found nothing. It was like she disappeared. I called their mom, and she was like, 'Honey, get on that plane and enjoy that trip; Miranda will be there eventually.' I believed her.

"I got on my flight without my wife and spent my first two days on my anniversary trip alone. The morning of the third day, I heard a knock at the door. I was so relieved. I had been calling Miranda the entire time, so the fact she was finally there made my heart smile, but when I opened the door, it was Maddy."

"Shut up."

"Yeah."

"How—"

"I still wonder how. Maddy was standing at the door, apologizing for her sister's behavior. She said that I deserved to enjoy my trip and not be worried about her, and she was there to make sure it happened."

"And..."

"We had a blast! Everything that was planned. Every meal, every tour, everything happened just as we planned for it to happen, and Madison made sure I smiled the entire time."

"If I was writing a movie, this would be a romance thriller, I think."

"Humph. Romance. So, that last night in Greece, we are sitting on the balcony, overlooking the entire town of Athens. It was gorgeous. Maddy looked at me and said, 'Aub, you are amazing.' This wasn't anything new or out of the ordinary, so I smiled and said, 'You know, Maddy, you are too.' It was like, in that moment, her guard came all the way down, and she even blushed a little bit. It made me feel something I hadn't felt for Maddy before. My thought was like, 'Damn, if my wife had been here, I know for sure we would have had at least two mental breakdowns, an argument, and we would have missed something because she couldn't get it together. This was a trip I couldn't have asked for, but it was given to me, and I appreciate her so much. That was the trap."

"What was?"

"Her ability to make me see her in a light that would let her in."

"Understood."

"That night she kissed me for the first time. That's all that happened."

"You told me all of that, and that's not when the affair started? I'm sick of you."

"That's where you're wrong. That's exactly where the affair started. I was hooked in that moment, and it took three more years of secret conversations and stolen moments before we ever had sex and began to move as a couple."

"How the fuck do you move as a couple with your wife's sister?"

"Easy."

"Trifling."

"Miranda hates Madison. They are rarely in the same place at the same time. The birth of our children, Madison wasn't even allowed to come to the hospital because it would have triggered Miranda. It was easy to be somewhere and not get caught."

"But you did get caught."

"Not because she saw us."

"Then how?"

"You got Apple products?"

"No, I am an Android user."

"I can see that."

"Now who is judging who?"

"You started it."

"And I am about to finish it."

"My Apple products are all linked. Usually locked, but all linked. One day, I wasn't home, but I wasn't with Maddy either; we were just talking, and Maddy began talking about one of our sexual rendezvous. Unbeknownst to us, Miranda wasn't in the office that day; she was working from home. My Mac was going off, so when she looked to see what was going on, she could read each and every message that was coming through, and she did that for hours."

"Ouch."

"When I came home that night, she had my shit all packed up. Told me I had to go. I betrayed her, I betrayed our children, and I needed to go."

"She wasn't wrong."

"I never said she was."

"So what did you do next?"

"I called Madison."

"And?"

"She told me it wasn't a good time."

"Ouch."

"When I pressed the issue, she told me that she was never really in love with me, and it was all a farce to get back at Miranda. Wished me a good life and hung up. I'd lost everything I cared about in a matter of thirty-five minutes."

"Damn. When did this happen?"

"Six months ago. That's what I mean when I say she was fucked up!"

Rookie, what do you think? Do you think Aubrey killed Madison? If you do, Skip ahead to page 116 and finish her interview. If you are certain that she has nothing to do with it, let's continue on to the next interview room.

DR. DIMITRIA KINCAID: THE THERAPIST

"Dr. Kincaid."

"Detective Shank."

"If you don't mind, I want to talk to you about a few more things."

"That's fine."

"I think I want to start with your experience with the phone call...and then delve more into your sessions with Madison."

"Okay."

"About what time did you get your call?"

"I think it was something like two fifty in the morning, give or take a few minutes, considering I was asleep."

"Wish I had been asleep myself."

"I rarely sleep, so for my sleep to be disturbed by something so unorthodox, definitely, is one for the books."

"Insomniac?"

"When you hear the horror stories I hear day in and day out, Detective, sleep becomes less and less attainable."

"Have you seen my job?"

"Touché."

"I recognize what you have to deal with because dealing with death in such terrible ways every day and seeing it for yourself is just as bad as listening to the horror stories. You read the books; I watch the movies."

"Excellent analogy."

"Thank you. I'm sorry. Continue."

"When I answered the phone, I heard heavy breathing. It was very odd. I said hello a few times, and then I hung up."

"They didn't say anything?"

"No."

"Okay."

"A few seconds later, the phone rang again. Sometimes, my patients call in the middle of the night, going through this or that, so I was inclined to answer again; it could save a life."

"Pun intended?"

"No."

"Sorry."

"This time, the heavy breathing was still present, so I said, 'If you are okay, just tell me. We can work through this.' The voice on the other end of the line said, 'I killed Madison.'"

"Just Madison?"

"Just Madison, and because they only said Madison, I didn't think we were talking about Madison McGhee right off that bat. There are probably 300,000 people in the world named Madison. I said, 'Why did you kill Madison, and where are you so I can come to you?' There were a few moments of silence, and then they said,

'I will meet you at the 700 block of 154th Street.' After that, the line went dead. I got dressed and got in my car. When I pulled up and saw Ten, I knew then the Madison they had been talking about."

"Did you recognize the voice at all?"

"No."

"Male? Female?"

"I say *they* because it could have gone either way. I do know it was not one of my patients. I had never heard that voice before. Ever."

"You said you treated both Ten and Madison, correct?"

"Correct."

"Ten is a lot."

"They both are."

"Looks to me, Ten was really upset for someone who had been fired."

"Is that what he told you?"

"Yes."

"Okay."

"Is there more to the story?"

"Ten is here, correct?"

"Yes."

"Then you can get his point of view from him; I am not needed for that. I am here to talk about Madison, the one who cannot speak for herself."

"You're right. Let's talk about Madison."

"Yes."

"From what I am gathering, Madison is a very complex individual."

"I would call her labyrinthine, but no need to play with semantics."

"Remind me to Google that word later."

"Intricate and confusing."

"Thank you, Dr Kincaid, I been up all night; brain was not ready for that one."

"Mm-hmm."

"What made her so intricate and confusing?"

"Reality is, Madison was a product of an upbringing that created two realities. That which was true to the world, and that which allowed her to be a functioning member of society without being a sociopath."

"Is this common in people who have such terrible childhood trauma?"

"Sometimes, and sometimes they just become sociopaths because that is easier."

"Interesting. So Madison lived in two realities?"

"Absolutely she did. In one reality, she was a boss bitch who got everything she wanted, and nothing stood in her way. In the other, she was a scared little girl who needed love and protection at all times."

"I assume you were aware of everything in her life?"

"I assume the same."

"Were you aware of her affair with Aubrey?"

Silence.

"I will take that as a no."

"When was this?"

"According to Aubrey, it ended about six months ago."

"Interesting. Very fucking interesting."

"I sense something here. Care to share?"

"Let me process that first. Is there anything else you need to ask me in the meantime?"

"I can figure something out."

"Please do."

"Madison's dual reality—is that something that can create enemies?"

"You can create enemies with one reality. Delusion doesn't create enemies; people create enemies."

"Okay."

"What we need to recognize about the creation of enemies is hate comes from love. If you have created an enemy, that person loved something about you at one point or another. They had enough care for you for that love to turn to hate and for them to want to harm you because of the inability of that emotion to go somewhere else."

"Okay, okay, okay. So it is safe to say that whoever killed Madison loved her at one point or another?"

"Loved her or had an affinity for her that was threatened."

"Explain."

"Another way to create an enemy is to threaten well-being or livelihood in some way, shape, or form, but to be able to do that, a person has to have let you in to a certain degree. You get let in when someone has an affinity, a caring for you."

"Love, like you just said?"

"No. There is a difference between love and affinity."

"Which is?"

"Love creates crimes of passion. I loved you, you hurt me, you caused me pain, so I am going to cause you pain. Affinity creates crimes of desperation. I let you in, you used me, you played me, you played with my life, so I am going to end yours."

"Have you ever been asked to be a part of an investigation?"

"No."

"Your insight is stellar. I am going to put you on our expert-witness list because this is something we can use later."

"No problem. I'll be around, I'm sure."

"From our perceptive, looking at the crime scene, this was definitely a crime of passion."

"Based on police standards, not psychological. I never saw the body, and I don't care to. Not my thing, but please explain why you think that."

"The condition of the body."

"Okay."

"To be able to stab someone so many times, you have to be intimate in some way. Usually, in crimes of passion, there is a stage of overkill because the passion doesn't allow the assailant to stop."

"There is no difference in that and a crime of desperation. The need to end the threat is just as powerful as the need to inflict pain because of hurt."

"I see."

"I've finished processing the Aubrey affair. Would you like to discuss it now?"

"Sure, I am learning a lot talking to you. The first question I have—"

"Let me start the questions this time, if I may."

"Oh, okay. Sure."

"Why did Aubrey say they ended?"

"She actually said that Madison told her that she was never really in love with her and that their entire relationship was fake and a vehicle for her to get back at Miranda for the years of mental abuse."

"And this ended six months ago?"

"Yes."

"How long had they been having the affair?"

"Sounds like roughly three years."

"So that is who she was talking about?"

"She talked to you about a woman she was with?"

"Yes, until she was with me."

"I'm sorry... What?"

"Yes, Madison and I had a brief but consistent affair."

"You were sleeping with Madison?"

"Yes."

"I didn't take you as a lesbian."

"I'm not."

"Okay..."

"Madison has a way of getting her way, no matter the obstacle, and sexuality wasn't a big enough obstacle for her."

"I'm sorry. I need to process now. So Madison was your client... *and* your lover. Isn't there some sort of law against that?"

"Yes."

"So you're a criminal?"

"Brash, but in this situation, I would have to say yes."

"Am I required to report you somewhere or something?"

"No. The relationship had ended before last night. It would be pointless now."

"I have to know how you got here and how it ended. You should have led with this."

"That would have been unnecessary."

"Spill it, Doc."

"I knew more about Madison than anybody else in her life. She felt safe with me. I gave her a sense of comfort and the space to be her true, authentic self. She didn't need to make a different reality when she was in my office. She didn't need to pretend to be the big boss or the mean girl; she just had to be Maddy. There was a difference between Maddy and Madison."

"What was the difference?"

"That dual reality thing I spoke about earlier. Maddy was soft and vulnerable, and that name was attached to familial roots. People in the business world called her Madison. If you didn't know her personally, Maddy did not exist."

"What did you call her?"

"Madison...until I didn't."

"Whatever that means."

"It means that until I was let in to that other side, she was Madison, and then one day I met Maddy. Madison began to work her charm to reel me in."

"Common theme here."

"I couldn't care less about her tactics with Aubrey."

"Okay then, continue."

"As I stated earlier this morning, I had been treating Madison for the better part of ten years. I knew everything about her. Top to bottom. While she was beautiful, she was conflicted, and I am straight, so there was never a danger of an 'us.' Then, one day, she came to the office when she didn't have a session. I was confused but whatever—after ten years, we are damn near friends. I didn't have a client at the moment, so it meant nothing. She looked me in my eyes and said, 'Tri.'"

"Who is Tri?"

"My name is Dimitria. That's the nickname people call me."

"Oh."

"Like I said, she looked me in my eyes and said, 'Tri, I want to make love to you. How does that make you feel?' I was speechless. No woman—or man, for that matter—had ever approached me in such a direct way. She was confident; she was domineering; she was all of a sudden attractive. Eventually, I responded and said, 'Maddy, we can't do that.' She challenged, 'Can't do it or you won't do it?' She had me there. Who would know? What was even more of a mind fuck—why was I so willing to consider it? To me, it was just sex. Nothing more."

"So you all had sex?"

"Yes, right there in my office. For hours."

"Hours?"

"Hours."

"And then what?"

"Weekly appointments. She would have her session and book the slots after, paid in full, and we would fuck all over that office."

"Oh wow, and when did this start?"

"Six months ago."

"When she ended it with Aubrey."

"I was sitting next to her when she got the call from Aubrey, but I didn't know it was Aubrey."

"You said it ended before last night. What happened?"

"The New York social scene is small. This is a known fact. Madison had started telling me she wanted more than just a sexual relationship with me. That was never something that was on the table for me. I was not about to dyke out for her."

"I'm unsure if you know, but you were having sex with her— you had already 'dyked out' for her. But continue."

"We ran into each other at a big networking event at the Apollo. A fundraiser for the restoration of the building. When she walked up to me, she tried to kiss me in front of people. I pushed her away and avoided her the rest of the night. What did she think this was? We hadn't discussed this; we hadn't made this a thing. Why would she think that was okay? I texted her while we were there and told her we needed to talk. We needed some clarity in the relationship."

"What did she say?"

"She told me she would meet me at my office after the event."

"Did you go?"

"Of course, I did. I needed to set the boundaries, so that this wouldn't happen again."

"So what happened when you got there?"

"When I arrived at my office, she wasn't there."

"That's disappointing."

"I'm not finished."

"My apologies."

"Rather than finding Madison waiting for me, there was a note taped to my door with a photo of us having sex. The note read, 'You fucked with the right one. You embarrassed me in public, and you will soon, too, be embarrassed in public. Kiss your career goodbye, bitch. See you at my session on Tuesday. Don't be late.'"

"Damn."

Rookie, what do you think? Do you think Dr. Kincaid killed Madison? If you do, Skip ahead to page 127 and finish her interview. If you are certain that she has nothing to do with it, let's continue on to the next interview room.

TEN BROADWAY: THE ASSISTANT

"Tren Ten Broadway."

"That's my name; don't wear it out!"

"You are a trip."

"You need a passport to swing my baby!"

"Speaking of swinging...did you ever sleep with Madison?"

"The fuck would you ask me that for? Have you seen me? She wishes...and ain't got the right toolbox to complete the job!"

"I just got to make sure at this point."

"Oh, tea? Spill it."

"None of your business."

"Then what you bring it up for?"

"Covering all my bases."

"Why I need to get back to my man, so I could get some of my bases covered."

"TMI, Ten, TMI!"

"Girl, why am I still here?"

"You go'n' be here until you tell me why you got fired. I'm just going to be honest with you. You are giving best actress in a homicide right now."

"Oh, you think I could act? I been thinking about getting in those Tubi movies or something."

"I was being facetious."

"What that mean?"

"I didn't mean you were literally trying to be in Hollywood, and let me just correct you for a moment. I am unsure what a Tubi movie is, but Tubi Original is just as good as a Paramount film. Tubi is not something to take lightly; don' disrespect the craft."

"Oh, you must got a movie on there or something?"

"I know people who work hard and get their movies picked up by Tubi. Just respect the damn craft, poser."

"You are rude. I love it!"

"Ten."

"You started with me; you told me I was about to get an award for my portrayal of a damsel in distress in a homicide."

"You know that's not a good thing, right?"

"Damn, really?"

"Really."

"So what you saying, Detective?"

"I'm saying the bitch who fired you is dead in the middle of the street, and you are acting like you lost one of your best friends, and that math ain't mathing!"

"LAWWWWWWWWWWWWWWWWWD, I forgot she was in the middle of the street just dead. Completely dead! Fuck! That's tragic."

"Do you really feel that way?"

"I do."

"Why? You have already said she was a bitch, and she fired you. Most people don't mourn people who treated them bad."

"She didn't treat me bad."

"I'm so confused."

"Me too. But we probably confused about two different things, chil'."

"What are you confused about, Ten?"

"It really stresses me out that Queen Bey wakes up to ugly-ass Jay-Z every morning. That doesn't make sense; she must not love herself!"

"Wow. Do you take meds?"

"All of 'em! Why? You got some in the back? I'll take two Percs and a diazepam, please and thank you."

"And you are also a drug addict?"

"Addict? No, baby. I like to feeeeeeel good. Okay. If you ain't got them, just tell me that; you ain't got to get no damn attitude and call me out my name. You know my name; just call me my name."

"Dr. Kincaid—"

"My knightess in shining armor."

"Is *knightess* the right word for that?"

"I don't know, but she's not a knight, so that works for me."

"Fine. How long has she been treating you?"

"About three years...about to be four on my birthday. Cancer!"

"How did you get referred to her?"

"Madison, duh."

"I figured, but I wanted to make sure."

"Mm-hmm."

"What made her refer you?"

"Girl, I needed somebody to talk to! My man had just woke up and left me!"

"Like woke up, literally, and left?"

"No, more like woke up a couple days and was feeling weird, and then decided he wanted to go back to his ex, the bitch that he was, and that he had moved too fast with me!"

"How long had y'all been dating?"

"About a month."

"And that devastated you to the point where you needed a shrink?"

"And shrunk, okay?"

"I don't even want to know. So you had this massive heartbreak—"

"Massive. Couldn't breathe, couldn't think, couldn't stop crying. I was a hot-ass, fucking mess!"

"And this wasn't going to work for the boss bitch that was Madison?"

"Not even in the least bit. Chil', she came to my apartment, opened them blinds, and told me, 'Get yo ass up. What the fuck is wrong with you?!'"

"Just like that?"

"Just like that. I hadn't been to work in days, and, baby, I smelled like it. I didn't even want to wash my ass anymore. So old Madison wasn't here for my stunts and shows, okay. She threw me in the shower, literally. Baby was strong, honey, 'cause you can see I ain't no little man! We got in her car, and she took me straight to Dr. Kincaid's office. We bust in there, and, chil', Dr. Kincaid had a whole patient in there! Madison looked at her and said, 'Fix this.' Dropped my ass off and told me to come to work when I was fixed."

"That's wild."

"I know, ain't it? It's one of my favorite stories with Maddy."

"Maddy?"

"Mm-hmm, Maddy."

"So is it safe to assume y'all had some sort of friendship, because I don't know too many bosses who would show up at their employee's—"

"Assistant. Put some respect on my title."

"You were fired; you have no title."

"Wow."

"I don't know many bosses who would show up at their ASSISTANT'S home and take them to get help after a breakup. That sounds very personable."

"I was needed in the office; I was fucking up the flow."

"So it was never really about you getting help. It was about her making sure business was taken care of."

"Yup!"

"Makes much more sense."

"Mm-hmm."

"How long was it before you went back to work?"

"I was a mess for about three months."

"You were a mess longer than the damn relationship?"

"My heart ached."

"Dramatic much?"

"How could you tell?"

"Call it a sixth sense."

"LAWWWWWWWWWWWWWWWWWWWWWD!"

"What now?"

Ten begins to lightly cry. "Bruce Willis. That dementia done got him."

"Ten."

"Yes."

"Come back."

"I'm right here."

"I'm about to ask you about the last big deal Madison was working on."

"The Ford Models account?"

"So you know about it?"

"Of course I do. I helped her secure it."

"How?"

"I'm offended at the damn question. I am good at my job!"

"The partnership was just recently announced in the news; you were FIRED six months ago."

"You keep using my current employment status against me, and I don't like it."

"You were."

"So?"

"How did you assist with the damn account, Ten?"

"You know nothing about the business."

"You are right, so enlighten me."

"Gladly. It takes months to acquire an account; it could take up to a year. It is a lot of courting and meeting and examples...and meeting again and dinner dates and happy hours. It takes a lot to make a client want to spend their money."

"This wasn't just money; this was going to be a billion dollar—"

"Ain't no *was*, honey; it is. Baby secured the bag; just 'cause she dead, the bag is still secured."

"This is a billion-dollar account. I'm sure it wasn't easy."

"Damn sure wasn't."

"So what did you do?"

"I was there every step of the way. From the moment the head of Ford walked into our office until the day she announced that we had inked the deal. I was there!"

"Okay, for shits and giggles, lay that out for me."

"You been to shits and giggles before?"

"Ten."

"Jail?"

"Yes."

"No, thank you."

"Tell me."

"Sure thing. When Ms. Ford walked into the office, Madison called me into the conference room immediately. The Ford Agency, as most of the world knows, represents models all over the world. These days, with Instagram and TikTok, the need to be represented isn't as big anymore. People get discovered on social media all the time, and while they do need representation to cross over into the bigger markets, the bigger agencies are losing out."

"Wow."

"I know. Crazy, right?"

"No."

"Then, wow what, girl? I ain't said nothing."

"That's the most coherent thing you've said to me today."

"Wow."

"My sentiments exactly. Continue."

"Anyways, Ford wanted to create social media ads that would target the influencers and bring in them influencers so that they didn't have to recruit; it would bring them clients, and they would be able to stay relevant. Because Pride Ads was new and upcoming, Ford wanted to see what fresh ideas we would have for this type of campaign. We are a millennial-run company, so with that being said, there is a certain edge that comes with us and an understanding about Gen X that was alluring to Ford."

"I could see that."

"Yeah, me too. I was there"—deep sigh—"anyways, Madison and I immediately went to work."

"Okay, what was the first step?"

"Research. We needed to know if there was anyone else out there doing what Ford was asking. And if there was, what did it look like?"

"Did you find anything?"

"Nope, so that meant we had free rein to knock this shit out the damn park and make some moneyyyyyyyy."

"Okay."

"Every night after work, we would go down to Evolve bar, and we would come up with ideas, just bouncing things off each other, creating designs, editing designs, and doing it all over again. And throughout that time, we were still meeting with Ford. Giving updates and ensuring that they knew we were serious about taking this innovative step in advertising."

"Okay, okay, I like where this is going."

"Right, so this lasted until about a month or so before my departure."

"Fired."

"Say it again."

Silence.

"Like I was saying, this lasted until about a month before my departure. That last month, I was damn near living with Maddy. You see, the idea she went with was one of mine, so I needed to be there throughout the development so that there was nothing missed."

"Makes sense. What was it?"

"Modeling 2.0. It would be a fully social media campaign that took video and futuristic images mixed with images of the past and lured the influencer in to be the new Beverly Johnson. Images of Beverly, Iman, Tyra, Naomi..."

"All Black?"

"No, some of those White girls were in it too, but I don't know they names like that; that wasn't for me to figure out."

"Okay..."

"Mm-hmm. The mash-up would be powerful, dynamic, and target everyone who thinks they can make it to the next level. It was a crazy mock-up. We watched it for hours and tweaked, and tweaked some more, and watched it. Came up with over twenty-five variations of the first rollout, and then a complete plan for over a year worth of advertising. I had even convinced Madison to reach out to some of the older models; this way, we are bringing them back into model work, showing the younger generation that it can be forever. Beauty is forever."

"Nice slogan."

"How did you know that was the slogan?"

"It has been announced, remember?"

"Oh yeah. Well, I came up with that too. That was the final piece of the puzzle—'Beauty is Forever, Ford Modeling Agency.'"

"You were right."

"I'm always right, but what about this time?"

"You were good at what you do. I'm sold, and I'm not even in the industry."

"I *am* good at what I do."

"You are good at what you do."

"When I left Madison's house that last night, we were both so excited. She was so proud of me. She said to me, 'Ten, how does it feel to have made your first million in commission?' I was crazed. A million dollars. Like, I was making maybe 150K a year, but I hadn't solely created an ad ever. I was going to make a one-million-dollar commission as soon as Ford signed the papers."

"You would make only one million; isn't she netting 500?"

"We are getting to that."

"Oh."

"The next morning, I walked into the office at my usual time—which is before anyone else since I run it—and I see everyone in the office celebrating. I was ready to party. And then I get pulled to the side. One of the girls said to me, 'Hey, what are you doing here?' And that shit didn't seem right or sit well in my shanana, so I said, 'I work here, and this is my celebration too. I secured this deal.' Her face told me everything I needed to know. Madison walked up and handed me an envelope. As of 5:00 p.m. the damn day before, I had been terminated."

"What?"

"Everything she submitted had her name on it. She stole my idea, my commission, and fired me in front of everyone, and I had nothing to show for it."

Rookie, what do you think? Do you think Ten killed Madison? If you do, Skip ahead to page 139 and finish his interview. If you are certain that he has nothing to do with it, let's continue on to the next interview room.

MIRANDA MCGHEE: THE SISTER

"Miranda."

"What?"

"I'm sorry to hear that your wife and sister were having an affair. That had to be hard for you to deal with."

"Haven't I been telling you this entire time that my sister was born a bitch. This ain't the first time."

"I'm sorry, what?"

"Madison has attempted, or succeeded, to sleep with every woman I have ever been with. This ain't new; it's just new to you."

"That is kind of wild."

"It is my reality, Detective. You wondered why I hated my sister; it was far deeper than just what meets the eyes. Not only did she want to outdo me in everything, but she wanted everything that was mine."

"How many women of yours did she get?"

"Dozens."

"Damn."

"I actually thought that Aubrey was going to be different."

"Why do you say that?"

"Aubrey handled me different. She handled Madison different."

"Meaning?"

"We know my mental-health issues; she never held it against me. She worked through all of it. Every episode, every moment, she was there. It wasn't always easy, but we worked through it. No one before had ever loved me through the sickness. My wife loved me through the sickness."

"And Madison."

"She saw Madison as a little sister. She never blinked when Madison attempted to get to her. She loved me; that was all it was. I know Madison seduced her; I know *how* she seduced her. I just never thought Aubrey could be seduced."

"How do you know?"

"I'm sick, Detective, not stupid."

"I wasn't insinuating that you were."

"I've seen it happen so many times. So many women fell victim to it, but this time I fucked up and left the space."

"Greece?"

"Yeah, Greece."

"Tell me about it."

"You don't know anything about mental illness, Detective. It fucks with you. It fucks with your perception; it fucks with everything in your life. It fucks with how you handle life. My wife wanted a family. Shit, I wanted a family. As you know, two women can't naturally have babies."

"How do I know?"

"We already established you're a lesbian; let's not do that."

"Carry on."

"The process of getting pregnant was tedious and scary because, at the end of the day, there is no guarantee that it will happen. Money spent, time spent, and you could easily have to start that process all over again several times before you truly get what you want. To a person who is already battling daily with their mind, that's cumbersome. Then, the knowledge of my illness and the fact I could pass it on to my children. I wouldn't wish this on my worst enemy, but I am going to willingly put my children in jeopardy? That fucked me up, Detective."

"I can imagine."

"I had been married for five years. My sister hadn't infiltrated my life; she hadn't broken us up. I was in a healthy place in my relationship, and here comes this addition that could fuck up everything. I know Aubrey didn't understand. How could she? I volunteered. I said I would carry. It would be me. She deserved that. She'd passed the test. Maddy hadn't won; the least I could do was give Aubrey these babies. I knew that when we got back from Greece it was going to begin, and I panicked. I completely lost my mind. I couldn't gather myself. I was in a deep, deep depression, and she wanted me to go overseas and enjoy myself. I couldn't. I couldn't do it. I wanted to die, to be honest."

"Why didn't you just tell her?"

"How do you tell someone who loves you so much something so hard?"

"So you lie?"

"What did I lie about, Detective?"

"You weren't forthcoming with the information; that's a lie."

"I gave her babies!"

"But you didn't tell her why you didn't want to go to Greece."

"I didn't have the words."

"That's just as bad as a lie."

Silent tears roll down Miranda's face.

"Continue."

"I hid for two days. I was under the Brooklyn Bridge...deciding if when she came home, I would be alive or not."

"Deep."

"Then my mother called. She asked me where I was and told me that Aubrey was so worried about me. I couldn't tell her where I was, so I told her I just didn't want to go, and Aubrey was a big girl; she would be fine. My mother said, 'I'm gonna send your sister.' What was I going to say?"

"You were gonna say, 'Hell no, the fuck you ain't!' I'm sorry; that wasn't professional at all, but I am so serious. You knew Madison's capabilities, and you didn't protest?"

"Mental illness creates mental weakness."

"That should be a billboard. Did you ever think about going to Dr. Kincaid?"

Miranda rolls her eyes.

"Never mind."

"When I hung up with my mother, I sat there and cried because I knew my marriage was over. But then they came back, and everything was normal. Madison still hadn't taken my wife from me. Life was amazing! I had my babies, I had my wife, and we were living good. Mentally, I was doing better, and I didn't have the shadow of Maddy hanging over me; she wasn't even around like that."

"But aren't you why she wasn't around?"

"Yes."

"So you created that space."

"I did. I created it for my sanity!"

"You created a space for secrecy and deceit."

"I knew something was going on; I just didn't know with who."

"Explain."

"Come on, Detective, you are a woman—women, we know. We know when something is wrong. We get a feeling deep in the pit of our stomachs that we can't get rid of. It causes us to lose sleep if we don't acknowledge it. It causes us to lose our appetites if we don't feed it. We know something is wrong when there are no signs at all. That's the beauty of being a woman."

"You're right."

"Aubrey's behavior never changed, but her energy did. Someone was taking up a space in her life that I had once occupied, and while it wasn't something I could physically touch, it was something I knew to be true."

"How did you find out what was going on?"

"Are you an Apple user, Detective?"

"No, are you going to judge me too?"

"No. Not my phone—I don't care. I'm just asking. I assume Android—or Google, whichever—has the same system. All of your devices sync to make life easier."

"Somewhat."

"One day, I was home. I didn't want to go into the office, Things have been different since Maddy's lawsuit—and sometimes I get the stares because I am her sister—when I have nothing to do with any of it. I'm an attorney, just as they are, but sometimes it becomes too much for me, you know?"

"I get it."

"Anyways, I stayed home, and worked from home. Aubrey and I shared an office; it was big enough for us to have enough space to maneuver our careers."

"What does Aubrey do? I know she used to be in the military."

"She owns an online store—natural things for the skin. Very successful. I was so proud of her."

"This is a different side of you, Miranda."

"I, unlike my sister, wasn't born a bitch. I was made into one."

Silence.

"Anyways, I was home working, and usually Aubrey's Mac is off; she powers down. But this particular day it was just on Sleep. For the first few hours I was home, she got sporadic messages. Nothing to make me blink. I was preparing briefs, so it didn't disturb me. It wasn't until sometime after lunch that all of a sudden, the computer was going DING DING DING DING DING DING DING DING DING DING DING DING DING DING DING DING DING DING DING DING DING DING—"

"Okay, that's enough."

"You see how annoying that was?"

"Very."

"That's what I was hearing. So I got up, not because I wanted to see who she was talking to, but because I wanted to turn that shit off, down...something. When I went to hit the mouse, I saw my sister's name pop up. On the Mac, it shows you the message whether the computer is locked or not."

"I'm sure there is a setting that can change that."

"I'm sure there is too, but up until that moment, she hadn't needed to change that particular setting."

"What did the message say?"

"My sister said to my wife, 'If you leave her, I'll leave with you; pack our bags, don't say a word, and we can go far away from this life."

"Damn."

"I never saw my wife's responses, but I sat in her chair for almost two hours and read every conniving, manipulative word my sister said to my wife. Every empty promise. Every lie. Every sick and twisted sexual fantasy she claimed she wanted my wife to do to her. I saw it all, and I knew Madison was full of shit!"

"How?"

"I didn't just meet my sister! I ain't new to this! I'm true to this! Madison was leading Aubrey's dumb ass, by a string, straight to hell!"

"How did that make you feel?"

"Hurt, but not hurt for the reason you would think."

"I think you would be hurt because you found out she was cheating."

"I was hurt because I found out she was just like everyone else."

"Ah."

"Maddy had in fact won, and I had made myself believe that wasn't true. Everything that had always been true was still true, and Aubrey was just another pawn in Madison's game, and she wasn't smart enough to change the rules."

"That's deep."

"She had to go."

"You put her out?"

"Absolutely."

"You couldn't have worked through it?"

"Where was my sister going? I didn't know she would die. In my mind, there would always be a Madison, so how could I keep my wife *and* my sister?"

"Your sister wasn't even in your life."

"In my life or not, Detective, Madison is my sister. She has been my sister for thirty-five years. Nothing and no one could change that, not even this fucked-up death."

"Miranda, I truly don't know what to say."

"Do you still think I killed my sister?"

"I honestly don't know what to think. You have the motive to do so."

"Let me be clear. If I wanted to kill my sister, she would have been dead long before last night. Maddy has done some terrible things to me throughout the years, but nothing terrible enough to make me want to take her life. Life is not mine to take. I am not God. I am not our parents. I did not give her life, so who the hell would I be to take her life away?"

"That sounds good—"

"Let me take it a step further. My sister, my only sister, has never done anything to me worthy of her life. Whether you believe me or not, Detective, there is no blood on my hands."

"And you can prove this?"

"I already have."

Unfortunately, Rookie, Miranda was telling the truth. She did not kill Madison. Her alibi checks out, and the cell-phone towers confirm she was home the entire night last night. Go back to page 73 and make a better decision. Time is of the essence.

INTERROGATION ROOM 2
AUBREY WILLIAMS-MCGHEE: THE SISTER-IN-LAW

"I want to dive more into this breakup if you don't mind."

"You can't break up with someone you were never with."

"That's true, but at the same time, it's not."

"How you figure?"

"While you may have never been official, you were in a situationship. That is like a relationship, and when it ends, that's called a breakup."

"She said none of it was real."

"Was it real to you?"

"Yes."

"Then it was a breakup, Aubrey, and that's okay."

"Okay."

"Did you not see any signs of Madison not being genuine?"

"No."

"How? Where was your women's intuition?"

"Nothing about her changed until about two weeks before we got caught."

"What changed?"

"Her availability was different; her tone was different; she seemed preoccupied when we talked. I knew she was doing that big deal at work, so I attributed it to the fact that she as trying to land a billion dollars. She ain't have time for me in those moments."

"To you, it was work related."

"Yes."

"I pulled your phone records."

Silence.

"You didn't take the breakup well at all. You called Madison several times over the last six months, and you also texted her a lot."

"I did."

"But you don't think it was a breakup?"

"I was hurt, I'm still hurt, and now I will never get closure."

"People usually do not need closure from something that wasn't a breakup."

"I had fallen in love with Maddy."

"What about Miranda?"

"I love my wife!"

"You are going to sit her and look me in my pupils and tell me you not only were in love with your wife's sister, but in love with your wife too?"

"I said I *loved* her."

"So you were not in love with Miranda?"

"Have you ever been in love, Detective?"

"Too many times to count."

"Then you know that being in love comes in waves. You may always love a person, but being in love comes with if you like them in that moment or not, the status of the relationship, intimacy—so many factors contribute to being in love."

"I can subscribe to that."

"So to say I wasn't in love with Miranda is subjective."

"Understood. But it is safe to say you believe you can love more than one person at one time?"

"Yes."

"How?"

"Love isn't a one-of-a-kind piece of paper that when you give it out, no one else will ever have that again. That's like asking a child, 'How could you possibly love your mother *and* your father? You have to pick one.' That's insane. Those are two different relationships and two different loves. The same thing comes with romantic love. Those were two different relationships with two different loves. Both of which can exist in the world."

"I never thought of it like that."

"Many don't, but it is real, Detective. I loved both of them. I just loved them different."

"Can I read you the last text you sent Madison, which happened to be last night?"

Silence.

"I'll take that as a yes."

> *Maddy, this will be the last time that I ever contact you. I apologize in advance for anything you may feel as a result of this, but this is something I need to do. I hope you understand that emotionally I feel truly*

bogged down, and I need to tell you the things in my heart so my heart will be free. Freedom is something I refuse to take for granted, and you shouldn't either. I love you; this is not a surprise; this isn't a revelation; this is a reality. I've held on to parts of our love, selfishly, and I tend to find myself remembering that time in life, which isn't this time in life. If that makes sense, which is what keeps my energy connected to yours. I relive our moments, our laughter, and our physical exchanges as if they are moments in the present rather than remnants of memories. I don't know what energy and connections mean. I haven't figured it out yet, but I know the strength of viewing things in relation to a whole. When materials combine in such a complementary manner on their own, they serve no purpose, they have no meaning, but together they leave us breathless and at one with the universe. I don't know what the universe has set for me and my feelings and my life, but I no longer want to force into the universe my selfish feelings for you. I want to release you from my burden. I will love you the rest of my life, but you don't deserve it, and neither do I, and if you died, I wouldn't cry because you never loved me anyway.

Silence.

"That is a lot, Aubrey."

"I'm ashamed, considering how the night ended."

"Anything you want to tell me?"

"Are you asking me if I killed Maddy?"

"I'm asking you if there is anything you want to tell me."

"No."

"Then I will save the other question until I feel it needs to be asked."

"Okay."

"What made you send this?"

"Self-reflection."

"Take me through that self-reflection."

"I was sitting in my hotel room in silence."

"Hotel?"

"I told you that Miranda put me out."

"You been living in a hotel for the last six months?"

"Yes."

"I need to see your website because that business must be amazing."

"I am very financially stable and no longer paying a mortgage on a place I am not living."

"Makes sense. Continue."

"I sat in the room, and I thought about everything. I thought about how she treated me, I thought about how she handled me, I thought about what she said to me, and, most importantly, I thought about what my actions had done to Miranda and my children. I knew I needed to release Maddy so healing could begin. Not just for me. But whatever Maddy could have been thinking, if anything at all, she hadn't responded to any of my messages, so I felt this message wouldn't be treated any different."

"So you tell her, if she dies, you won't cry?"

"A bit dramatic, I admit, but I lied."

"What did you lie about?"

"I cried as soon as I got the phone call."

"Yes, the phone call, I'm glad you brought that up. We hadn't had a chance to talk about it. What time did you get your call?"

"Had to be around two thirty or so. Don't you have my phone records?"

"We are currently processing the call log; it was easy to print the text messages from your iCloud. Thank Apple when you get a chance, will you?"

"Shady, you need some coffee, Detective?"

"I probably do, and I will have some after I finish these interviews."

"Sounds like you need it now."

"Please finish your story, and don't worry about my caffeine intake."

"Anyways, I was in my hotel room, and, honestly, I hadn't too long ago sent Maddy that text. I sent it to her about 1:00 a.m., so when my phone started ringing, I thought it was her."

"If she hadn't responded in all that damn time, why would she respond to that text after that ignorant-ass last line?"

"Hopeful heart, I guess."

"Which means you weren't really done. You sent that shit to get a reaction out of her and hoped you succeeded."

"This could be true."

"It is, but continue."

"I was watching TV when my phone started ringing. I will say, now, my feelings were kind of hurt when it wasn't her voice on the other end of the line. When I answered, I said, 'You're finally ready to face me like a woman?' The voice on the other end said, 'She will never face you again.' It shook me to my core. I sat up in the bed, and I was like, 'Excuse me?' After some moments of absolute silence, the voice said, 'Madison is dead. I killed her.' I didn't know if this was her playing, trying to tell me she was dead to me, because that's some shit she would say. I didn't know what to make of it, so I said, 'Maddy, stop playing; grow up so we can end this like adults.'"

"Nothing about the call up until that point scared you?"

"Naw, Maddy was weird like that. You know there is an app where you can change your voice, right?"

"No, I didn't, but you seem to know."

"Most people know. There are several apps on the market, and the ones you pay for can make you sound like anything or anybody. Maddy had a few of them, so it was nothing for me to think she was pranking me."

"You are telling me you are the only person who knew Madison and knew she had these apps? Why has no one else mentioned it to me?"

"I keep telling you; our relationship was different. Of the people you have here, none of them would have experienced that side of Maddy."

"You aren't making sense, Aubrey."

"How am I not making sense?"

"Madison didn't even want you. She played you like a damn PS5 and left you in the street to die—not literally, but you know. How could she do all of that and then care enough to be silly and be herself with you?"

"You ever lost yourself in a moment?"

"Depends on what we are talking about."

"Even the biggest master of deception cannot deny fun and a true connection. The things I talked about in that final text—nothing we did could change the chemistry between us. So in those moments when we were just enjoying our time—no sex, no creeping, just Madison and Aubrey—her guard was down. She was child-like. She was funny. She wanted to prank people and not live in this adult world where she had to be Madison McGhee. She just wanted to be Maddy. Miranda didn't get that side of her. Miranda didn't want to get to know the adult Maddy. She was so stuck on everything that had happened—"

"Madison ain't no saint there."

"I won't say she was, but had Miranda given her a chance, I believe she would have stopped her revenge circuit."

"Understood."

"Ten never got that side of her either. He works for her. She can't be that person; she would be taken advantage of."

"What about Dr. Kincaid?"

"Isn't that just her shrink?"

"Understood."

"I'm just saying, why would she show her that side?"

"She showed her every other side."

"What does that mean?"

"In sessions, you have to be vulnerable."

"Oh, I thought you meant something else."

"Like what?"

"Nothing, never mind. Can I finish the story?"

"Go ahead. I ain't stopping you!"

"You defiantly interrupted me, asking me about the app!"

"You're right. My apologies. Continue."

"I kept saying, 'Stop playing, Maddy,' and the voice kept saying, 'She's dead. I killed her.' So I said. 'Fine. Prove it.' Then the voice calmly said, 'Go to the 700 block of 154th Street, and see for yourself,' and then the phone went dead. That was when I got scared."

"What made that part different?"

"It felt different."

"Women's intuition is a theme."

"Call it what you must, but soon as I grabbed my keys, I felt this overwhelming sense of despair and grief."

"But you didn't know she was dead."

"My heart knew; my mind did not want to accept it."

"Aubrey, I am going to be honest with you. I saw you at the scene."

"I saw you at the scene too."

"I mean I saw how you were looking at Madison."

"How was I looking at her?"

"You had a look of detest, not the look of someone who was grieving."

"I cried all the way there. I cried my heart out. I screamed. I banged my steering wheel, and I asked God for strength. Then I pulled up. I saw Miranda getting out of her car, I saw the police tape, and it all became real. Then I saw Maddy lying there. I was so mad at her!"

"Why?"

"Because if she would have just talked to me, maybe I could have saved her. Maybe I could have said something to prevent this from happening to her."

"So glare at her lifeless body?"

"Have you ever seen somebody you loved lying in the street, half dressed, bloody as hell, and dead?"

"No."

"Then talk to me about my faces when you have to face that shit yourself!"

"I still am not sure I believe you."

"What are you trying to say, Detective?"

"I just state facts."

"And what are the facts?"

"The facts are Madison caused you to lose everything—your home, your family, and your mind. You spent six months attempting to get her to speak to you, and on the night she was murdered, not only did you send her a text about releasing her, but you also told her that if she were to die, you wouldn't cry. That all seems like you could have done something you regret, don't you think?"

"Naw, I ain't go'n' agree to that."

"Aubrey, did you kill Madison?"

"Absolutely not, Detective."

"Are you sure?"

"I am beyond sure. I just told you I was in love with Madison. If I am guilty of anything, it would be being in love with my wife's sister. That's the only crime I've committed here."

"You are telling me nothing about what Madison did infuriated you?"

"Of course, it did."

"To the point of homicide?"

"No."

"Crimes of passion come out of extreme love, are you aware of that?"

"I don't give a fuck about that!"

"What do you give a fuck about?"

"The fact that one of the women I love is lying in a body bag right now in the coroner's office. I give a fuck about the fact that my wife, my mother-in-law, and my kids have to bury someone so dear to them. I give a fuck about the fact that someone hated her soooooooooo much that they felt this was the answer."

"Can you prove to me you didn't do this?"

"I already have."

Unfortunately, Rookie, Aubrey was telling the truth. She did not kill Madison. Her alibi checks out, and the cell-phone towers confirm she was home the entire night. Go back to page 84 and make a better decision. Time is of the essence.

DR. DIMITRIA KINCAID: THE THERAPIST

"Dr. Kincaid, may I call you Tri?"

"No."

"Okay."

"Why do you deem it necessary to call me Tri?"

"We have been here together a long time; we are just about friends, aren't we?"

"No."

"Enough said. Are you ready to continue with this interrogation?"

"Interrogation or interview?"

"It could go either way; that depends on you."

"I'm unsure what that may mean, but I am also not interested in asking more questions."

"Don't worry. We will both find out shortly."

Silence.

"What did you think about the note that Madison left on your door?"

"I thought that that sociopath I spoke about earlier had finally reared its head."

"Then what did you do?"

"Naturally, I called her. I wanted to know where her mind was, what she was thinking, and how she could have possibly believed that this course of action fit the circumstance."

"What was the circumstance?"

"Did we not just discuss this?"

"We did."

"So what exactly am I answering if you know the circumstance?"

"Sometimes circumstances change over time."

"What time, Detective?"

"The hours we have been sitting here."

"Nothing changed."

"Humor me. What was the circumstance?"

"Madison and I were simply having sex. There was no circumstance. It was scheduled; it was planned. Madison wanted a relationship with me, a straight woman. I did not want a relationship with her. My patient, client— however you see her—and a lesbian woman. That was the circumstance, and nothing you say or do will alter that reality."

"You spoke earlier about Madison's dual realities."

"Yes, I did."

"Is it safe to say that as you were engaging in this 'circumstance,' you were playing into her dual reality?"

"I don't believe I understand what you are asking me."

"You said Madison wanted a relationship with you."

"Yes."

"Which reality was that? Madison or Maddy?"

"The conquest of the straight woman was Madison. The need to be loved and nurtured by anybody was Maddy."

"As her caregiver—"

"I am not a caregiver, Detective."

"Are patients not in your care when you are dealing with them?"

"They are."

"Now, correct me if I'm wrong; the definition of a caregiver is someone who regularly looks after a sick—or in this case, mentally unwell—person."

"I never said Madison was mentally unwell."

"What was she?"

"She was a functioning adult in society that had childhood trauma that caused her to display symptoms of borderline personality disorder; however, she was not, and had never been, diagnosed with the disorder."

"Yes, borderline personality disorder. I have the DSM-5 handy. The definition of this disorder is 'a pervasive pattern of instability of interpersonal relationships, self-image, and affects, and marked impulsivity beginning by early adulthood and present in a variety of contexts.' Does this sound like the same thing you just described seeing in Madison?"

"It does."

"So is it safe to say that she had this disorder; you just didn't do your job in diagnosing and treating her for it? So you sent her into the world as two different people navigating a mental condition that was undiagnosed?"

Silence.

"I will take it even a step further. Her sister is manic-depressive—"

"The term *manic-depressive* is dead. Miranda is bipolar."

"I thought you did not treat Miranda?"

"I *don't.*"

"Then how do you know her diagnosis?"

"I never said I *never* treated her."

"Oh, so Miranda was one of your patients as well once upon a time?"

"Once upon a time."

"Noted. Back to my original point, is mental illness hereditary, Dr. Kincaid?"

"In some cases, it can be."

"That's what I thought. Do you watch true-crime documentaries?"

"Not something I am interested in."

"Such a shame."

"Why is that?"

"Last weekend, I happened to be home, doing nothing. I turned on my TV, and there was a docuseries playing on HBO called *Six Schizophrenic Brothers*. It was fascinating. Of the twelve siblings in this family, six of them were schizophrenic, and the parents were never mentally ill. They just created fucked-up kids."

"What is your point, Detective?"

"Well, looks like, to me, if you knew Miranda had a mental illness, you would have been more careful with Madison, considering she, too, could have been mentally ill."

"In my care—"

"Just want to note you are acknowledging that you were her caregiver with that statement."

"In my care, Madison was thriving. She did not need to be medicated."

"Was she really?"

"Yes."

"Then why would you call her a sociopath if she was thriving. You are making me question that Columbia degree, Doc."

"All psychotic breaks are not the same."

"So you think you triggered a psychotic break?"

"No."

"Then what do you think, Doc?"

"I think that rejection caused a psychotic break in her."

"Humor me again and explain what a *psychotic break* means."

"A psychotic break is when a person loses touch with reality because their mental well-being is on a decline. This could signal another underlying illness—"

"Such as borderline personality disorder. Got it."

"Or it can be temporary and caused by stressors that the person's mental capabilities at the time cannot process."

"I see you go'n' stick to that."

"I am."

"I am interested in what happened when you talked to Madison after you found the note."

"I didn't talk to her."

"Excuse me?"

"She didn't answer my call."

"So what happened?"

"I had to wait until I saw her at her session on that following Tuesday."

"Why didn't you just say that? You made it sound like you never spoke to her again."

"No, I simply said she never answered my call that night, which is the night you were asking me about."

"Semantics, but whatever. Continue."

"She showed up for her standing appointment like nothing had ever happened. I asked her, 'Is there something you think we need to discuss?' and she said to me, 'Nothing that we need to discuss now.' Her tone alerted me that she meant more than what she was saying, so I kept asking questions. 'When would be the time for us to talk about it?' She said, 'In front of the psychology board.'"

"She was going to report you?"

"She then pulled out a folder. In the folder was every single time we had had sex. Detailed and outlined. She had photos, and she even had recordings from her booking the appointments after her weekly sessions."

"Damn."

"She said to me, 'Tri, I loved you. I trusted you, and you betrayed me. If you and I are not together, I will ruin you, and everything you ever thought you could or would touch will turn to shit.'"

"Did you believe her?"

"I did. I saw it in her eyes; any mental stability that she once had was gone, and it was because I triggered her."

"Then what happened?"

"I slowly sat down next to her and said, 'Maddy, you know we can't be together.' And she began to cry. She said, 'I have already sent one photo to the press.' Then she showed me the photo that she had sent."

"What was it?"

"No faces could be seen. She said she told them to stay tuned; a local psychiatrist had seduced her mentally ill patient, and more information would follow."

"Shit."

"Then we had sex."

"What?"

"It was the only thing I could do."

"How?"

"If I hadn't, she would have ruined me."

"So fucking her—that was your solution?"

"In that moment, yes."

"When did all of this start happening?"

"We were about three months in when the Apollo event took place."

"Then you slept together how much longer after that?"

"Until last Tuesday."

"What happened last Tuesday?"

"Madison arrived for her standing appointment, and my boyfriend was there."

"Pardon?"

"You heard me, Detective."

"Y'all is some of the cheatingest... You had a boyfriend this entire time?"

"Yes."

"You had a boyfriend, and you were sleeping with Madison?"

"Yes."

"Wow."

"What about this is hard for you to grasp, Detective?"

"You don't think that, not only were you dead-ass wrong for sleeping with someone in your care, but you had a relationship that you were stepping out on?"

"She was a woman; it wasn't cheating."

"Y'all straight women kill me with that shit!"

"I don't know what you mean."

"I doesn't even matter. I imagine she acted a damn fool when she saw this man there with you."

"She walked in, she saw me kiss him goodbye, and when I looked up, she was gone."

"That was disappointing."

"I'm sorry that my life story wasn't entertaining enough for you, Detective."

"Oh, it's entertaining; just, that particular point fell short. What happened after that?"

"On Wednesday, I got a call that I was under investigation for improper conduct with a patient."

"Who did you get the call from?"

"The American Board of Psychiatry and Neurology. The local chapter in New York, of course."

"What had she done?"

"Madison sent the entire file, including a photo of me and my boyfriend kissing, to them. I was immediately placed on suspension. My license, my practice, and everything could be snatched from me at any moment. They had all the proof. The investigation was routine, and they needed to interview me."

"When were you interviewed?"

"That Friday."

"A few days ago?"

"Give or take."

"How did that go?"

"They asked me what happened, and I told them."

"Well, I hope you didn't tell them like you told me, because you were evasive as hell."

"They had it in their hands. What was I supposed to say?"

"Understood."

"Did you have contact with Madison after that?"

"Of course, I did."

"When?"

"Last night when I killed her."

"What?"

"Last night...when I killed her."

Silence.

"I sat in front of her house for three days. Madison ruined me. She took what we had and put it on display for the world to see. She made a mockery of me."

Silence.

"So I made a mockery of her. I sat, and I waited. The longer it took for her to come home, the more detailed my plans got. Had she come home Friday night, she may still be alive, but she didn't. Friday night came and went. Saturday night came and went. Sunday night came and went. Just when I thought about giving up, her car came flying down 154th Street. I watched her get out of her car. Carefree, she was so free. She had no worry in the world. That bitch walked to her door like she had the right to still be free."

Silence.

"As she pulled her key out, I said, 'Did you think you would never see me again?' She paused before she turned around, and then she turned around and smiled at me. The bitch smiled at me. I should have cut her fucking lips off."

Silence.

"She looked at me and said, 'I actually looked forward to the moment we saw each other again.' And then she invited me into her home. She thought I was there to have sex. She actually thought that after she ruined me, I would want her. She even said that she figured once I lost everything, boyfriend included, that I would need her, and we could be happy together."

Silence.

"We never made it into the house. I touched the small of her back, and I smiled back and said, 'Take a ride with me first.' She was dumb enough to oblige. We got in my car, she leaned over to kiss me, and I stabbed that bitch in her stomach. I stabbed her, and I turned the knife so that it would destroy whichever organ I touched. Then I kept stabbing her as she looked at me—like she usually did—like I was going to be her forever. Then I drove a little farther up the street, and I grabbed my gun. I ripped her clothes off so I could I see what I had done to her, and then I shot her. Right there in the car. It was quiet; silencers are amazing. And you know what, Detective?"

Silence.

"She never screamed. She never made a sound. I waited for her to bleed out, and when I realized her eyes would never close, I tried to close them, but unlike the movies, that shit didn't work. Every time I tried to close them, they popped back open. She kept looking at me, even long after her heart stopped bleeding. I drove a little farther once she was dead, and I threw her ass out the car. I put her wallet and shit on the sidewalk, and I went and dumped the car that I stole to do all of this in, in the Hudson River."

"Dr. Dimitria Kincaid, you are under arrest for the murder of Madison McGhee. You have the right to remain silent. Anything you say can and will be used against you in a court of law. You have a right to an attorney. If you cannot afford an attorney, one will be appointed for you."

Congratulations, Detective! I knew I liked you when I first saw you. Something about you made me say, "That right there is going to be a great detective one day." You solved the case. You saw right through Dr. Kincaid's façade. Pat yourself on the back and head to page for 149 your debriefing, Detective.

TEN BROADWAY: THE ASSISTANT

"Ten, Ten, Ten."

"You like me, huh, Detective Shank? I know you do, girl; ain't no need in hiding it, chil'. I see it all in your eyes. No, I don't date women, but after all of this blows over, and you left me out of here, we can go eat. I like to eat."

"I'm not going anywhere with you, Ten, and I barely like you."

"That's the thing though; you didn't say you didn't like me. You said you barely like me, and that means you like me just a little bit!"

"Whatever. Madison stole your idea, your money, and your job."

"Chil', tell me about it."

"I'd rather *you* tell me about it."

"I did."

"I need some more details in your story."

"Oh, you want me to add a little bit of Lawry's."

"Seasoning salt?"

"Mm-hmm."

"Um, sure."

"Okay, girl. So when she told me I was fired, I needed a reason. Because, baby, the night before, we was working 'til 1:00 a.m., so how in the hell monitored by sweet Black Baby Jesus could I have been fired the day before at 5:00 p.m.? It was some hours that were not accounted for in that."

"Did you ask her?"

"You bet your sweet ass I did!"

"And she said?"

"Nothing, chil'. She walked away! That thang there was a cold piece of work. God rest her cold-ass soul."

"Wait. So you don't know why you got fired?"

"Nope."

"Not at all?"

"Nope."

"You telling me that she took all of that from you, and you don't know why?"

"Nope."

"What?"

"That ain't what I said."

"But you just said—"

"I said I didn't know why she fired me; I didn't tell you I didn't know why she did what she did."

"Then tell me why she did what she did."

"I heard—"

"You heard?"

"Yes, I heard that she was trying to start a little fling or something with one of those Ford executives, and she needed to impress her smooth out of her panties, so having my name on it would have messed up her chances of chasing that cat, if you get my drift."

"Where did you hear that?"

"Oh, the girls in the office talk, honey."

"What else did the girls in the office say?"

"They said that she had to fire me so there was no trace of my input on the campaign. The thing is, we always worked on that shit off the clock. She was a smart one. LAWWWWWWWDDDDDDDDDDDDD, I can't believe she gone. JESSUSSSSSSSSSS, somebody done took her from us. LAWDDD, WHY?"

"Why do you even care? She fucked you over!"

"So."

"So?"

"So."

"So you just cool with being fucked over?"

"Naw, I never said that."

"The more I talk to you, the less and less you make any damn sense!"

"I make cents and dollars, baby; you better ask somebody about me!"

"Ten, I am not afraid to arrest you."

"What will be my charges, Detective?"

"Excessive bullshit."

"I ain't never heard of that in no courthouse!"

"How many times have you been at the courthouse, listening to charges?"

"I go by and visit every now and again."

"I bet you do."

"Ain't got to bet on it when I'm telling you the truth."

"I'ma run your name when I get out of here."

"You know how to spell it, right?"

Silence.

"T-R-E-N-T-E-N-A-L-O-Y-S-I-U-S-B-R-O-A-D-W-A-Y."

"Thank you, Ten."

"You're welcome, girl."

"Can we get back to the situation at hand?"

"Absolutely."

"So you weren't mad that Madison did that to you?"

"Not really."

"Why not?"

"Pride Ads was one of her dreams. She had become mad successful, and if my idea was going to take her to the next level, whether people knew my name had anything to do with it or not, I was still a part of that elevation, and I'm grateful for that."

"And what about the money?"

"Baby, do you know who my daddy is?"

"Who?"

"Will Smith!"

"You lying."

"I know."

"What your daddy got to do with this?"

"Nothing, I just love Will Smith real bad."

"You ain't mad that girl didn't give you your million-dollar commission?"

"No, I ain't mad that that girl didn't give me my million-dollar commission!"

"Are you mocking me?"

"Are you mocking me?"

"Ten."

"Detective."

"Are you always like this?"

"I am, girl."

"Ain't you sleepy?"

"Been sleepy long time ago."

"And you acting like this?"

"Had I got a nap, I'd be in rare form."

"This ain't rare form?"

"This is mild form; I need a bed, honey."

"I would have fired your ass too if you are more than this on a usual basis!"

"You really are rude. I love it!"

"Is there anything else you can tell me about Madison?"

"What you want to know?"

"You worked for her."

"Did."

"Who did she have dealings with; who might have wanted to kill her?"

"Everybody."

"Everybody?"

"Yeah."

"What?"

"I told you that girl was a bitch. I wasn't playing with you. She was cutthroat. She let go of a whole damn department; they all wanted her dead. She fired me, but I didn't want her dead; just make sure you note that in your little papers over there. Madison's business practices were unorthodox, to say the least."

"Spell *unorthodox*."

"UN-OR-THO-DOCKS. Don't play with me, Detective. I know how to spell the words I am using."

"You sure do."

"Mm-hmm."

"Do you have a list of people who you know she did wrong in business?"

"I keep all my records. I know every single person that she fired, hired, fucked, sucked, fucked over, under, and in between."

"Excellent. We are getting somewhere. First name."

"Oh, I don't know it by heart."

"What?"

"What made you think that I would know that by heart?"

"The way you were saying it was like you knew it inside and out."

"I said I keep all my records. At home. Where I need to be."

"I'm so sick of you."

"I be sick of me too, chil'."

"Can you get someone to send them? A picture or something."

"Ain't nobody in my house. Can't nobody live with me again until I get married. Men don't know how to act."

"Women either."

"Give me some, girl"—extending his hand—"'cause I know that's the truth. Oh, you gone leave me hanging? I see you."

"Have we talked about the phone call yet?"

"Nope."

"Tell me about the call."

"Somebody called me and told me Madison was dead."

"That much I know."

"Then what you want to know?"

"The story, Ten. What happened; where were you? What did they say? This is a murder investigation, Ten; act like you are aware of that."

"LAWWWWWWWWWWWWWWWWWWWWWD."

"Don't start that shit."

"When I'm done telling you the story, will you let me cry and mourn in peace?"

"Yes."

"Thank you."

"You have to tell the story for the story to be done, Ten."

"Oh, you right."

"Tell the story now, Ten."

"I was home watching a good Lifetime movie! Do you watch Lifetime, Detective? You look like you watch Lifetime."

Silence.

"Anywhooo, I was watching the movie, and I was nodding off. You know how it is to be old, and I nodded straight into a coma. Mouth open, drooling, I was sleeping good, and that phone scared the dog shit out of me! I popped up so damn quick."

"Do you remember what time it was when they called you?"

"Round about two forty, I reckon."

"You reckon?"

"I turned the movie on about ten thirty, and then I was probably comatose by eleven thirty. I had had one dream, so I must have

146

been in REM sleep for the second time, which takes about ninety minutes in the sleep cycle. So, yeah, I'ma go with two forty in the morning, Alex."

Silence.

"You don't watch *Jeopardy*?"

"Alex Trebek is dead, and been dead, so don't start your shit. Just finish the damn story."

"Meany. I answered the phone; I said, 'Hello,' and they said, 'Madison McGhee is dead.' And I said, 'I know you fucking lying.' And they said, 'I'm not.' And I said, 'Well, who killed her?' And they said, 'I did.' And then I said, 'Well, why for you killed her?' And they said, 'You will find out.' So I said, 'Ooooh, tea. Spill it.' And they said, 'Go to the 700 block of 154th Street, and you will find out all the tea.' And then I said, 'Oh no, honey, I can't do that. I done took my bra off for the night. I'm in the house, baby.' And then they said, 'If you don't go right now, you go'n' be next.' So I said, 'Let me grab my keys.'"

Silence...

...silence...

...silence...

...and more silence...

"You never asked who you were speaking to?"

"Naw, why would I do that?"

"Somebody called you and told you that Madison was dead, and told you to go see, and then said if you didn't go, you would be next...and you never thought to ask who it was?"

"Nope."

"Ten, did you kill Madison?"

"Hell naw, I'm too pretty for prison!"

"Ten."

"Yes, baby."

"Get the fuck out of my presence...now!"

"Bye, girl!"

Unfortunately, Rookie, Ten was telling the truth. He did not kill Madison. His alibi checks out, and the cell phone towers confirm he was home the entire night. Go back to page 106 and make a better decision. Time is of the essence.

Congratulations, Detective! You have officially solved your first case. How does it feel? Man, I remember my first case back in the day. You know what I mean when I say "back in the day," don't cha?

Anyways, it wasn't as complicated as this one. I had a little homicide down in Brooklyn, and the dude who did it, he was like sitting down the street when we rode by. I noticed him when my partner and I rode by, and I looked at him; he wasn't paying attention.

"Hey, you think we should ask him if he saw anything?" I asked my partner because in my head the man on the street was too damn close to the scene of the crime not to know shit.

"He don't know shit."

"Ain't he right here at the scene of the damn crime?"

"Yeah."

"And it don't make sense to you to stop and ask him anything?"

"No."

I knew then I needed a new damn partner because his ass was about get me fired.

I went with him to the scene of the crime, and I kept looking down the road. The dude was still sitting there! Ain't nobody just sitting outside and it's been a murder in the neighborhood. They go'n' come watch; they go'n' go in the house; they go'n' do something other than sit on the stoop looking stupid.

I decided I was going to take myself down the street and ask some questions. Soon as I started walking, he started running.

"Perp on the run!" I screamed because had we stopped when I said the shit, I wouldn't be running down the damn street! I was so mad when I caught him! Come to find out, he killed the dude after a Madden game. People kill over anything. The world is just sick.

Tangent over. Back to you.

I like the way you handled yourself in there. You remained focused and steadfast in your detective skills while trying to figure out who had taken Madison's life. Each person was different, and they all had a reason to do it, but you were able to see straight through Dr. Kincaid, even though for me it was a toss-up between Miranda and Audrey. I knew Ten couldn't bust a damn grape, let alone commit murder, but we needed to talk to him anyways.

You even knew better than I did. That takes some skill, and I am proud of you. We have a lot of paperwork to fill out, so your job isn't done yet, but I do want to tell you a little bit more about Dr. Kincaid if you have a moment.

It's obvious she never received a call, but did you recognize how her recollection of the phone call was different than everyone else's. The assumption would be that she made the calls, so she should know exactly what the hell was said and how it went, but she didn't. She created a robot caller, but what she did not account for was, in her story, she mentioned heavy breathing. AI ain't that bright. The bot she created was able to react to certain prompts, which leads me to believe that Ten was half lying about his call, 'cause ain't no bot said to him that shit about tea, but maybe it did. I don't know. The doctor tripped herself up, but I believe she wanted to get caught. Had she never shown up, we would have never known about her. But she did, and we caught her. We did it. You did it. Now, go fill out your paperwork, and don't leave anything out! Good job. I'm going to take a nap!

SUPPLEMENTARY HOMICIDE REPORT

Within 30 days of the homicide incident, the chief law enforcement officer for an agency must submit a completed form to superiors.

REPORT ONLY ONE INCIDENT PER FORM- Report all homicides for this incident (case#) on this form.

*Agency ORI: _____ ***Agency Name:** _____

*Date of Incident: (mm/dd/yyyy) _____

*Incident/Case Number: _____ (8 characters)

☐ Yes ☐ No   The date given above is the actual incident date of the Homicide, and not the date the incident was reported.

*Was there a death in this incident?   ☐ Yes   ☐ No

Do any of the following apply to any victims of this incident, if so please check the box below.		
☐ A Death was a suicide	☐ A Death was from a heart attack or natural causes	☐ Death was due to traffic fatality
☐ Accidental Death Not from Negligence	☐ Death due to motor vehicular manslaughter	

If any death is checked above, do not report it on this form. It is not considered a homicide.

*Select Either <u>1a</u> or <u>1b</u> Homicide Type and Circumstances.

1a. ☐ **Murder and Non-negligent Manslaughter** *(Includes the reporting of "Justifiable Homicide")*	Definition: *The willful (non-negligent) killing of one human being by another.*

Up to <u>Two</u> Circumstances and ☐ Argument ☐ Assault on Law Enforcement Officer(s)
☐ Drug Dealing   ☐ Mercy Killing   ☐ Gangland (Organized Crime Involvement)
☐ Juvenile Gang   ☐ Lover's Quarrel   ☐ Domestic Dispute   ☐ Unknown
☐ Felony Involved Circle One   Rape, Robbery, Burglary, Larceny, Motor Vehicle Theft, Arson, Sex Offenses, Prostitution & Commercialized Vice, Narcotics/Drug Laws, Gambling, Human Trafficking/Commercial Sex Acts, Human Trafficking /Involuntary Servitude, Other Felony
☐ Other Circumstances

If "**Justifiable Homicide**" - check: ☐ Perpetrator Killed by Law Enforcement
☐ Perpetrator Killed by Private Citizen

Definition: The killing of a perpetrator of a serious criminal offense by a police officer in the line of duty;

or the killing, during the commission of a criminal offense, of the perpetrator by a private citizen.

1b. ☐ Negligent Manslaughter	Definition: *The killing of another person through negligence, with no willful intent.*

One Circumstance: ☐ Child Playing with Weapon   ☐ Gun Cleaning Accident
☐ Hunting Accident   ☐ Other Negligent Weapon Handling   ☐ Other Negligent Killing

*REQUIRED: Provide a Brief Narrative of the Homicide Situation Being Reported

(Enter Public Data Only)

*Select One Situation:

☐ Single Victim/Single Offender   ☐ Multiple Victims/Single Offender

☐ Single Victim/Unknown Offender or Offenders   ☐ Multiple Victims/Multiple Offenders

☐ Single Victim/Multiple Offenders   ☐ Multiple Victims/Unknown Offender or Offenders

* Required Fields   Page 1   Supplemental Homicide Form -R 1/1/2014

VICTIM/OFFENDER INFORMATION CODES

Age (Victim and Offender)	Sex	Race	Ethnicity
UB = Unborn Fetus - (Victim Only)	M = Male	W = White	H = Hispanic or Latino Origin
NN = Under 24 hours - (Victim Only)	F = Female	B = Black or African American	N = Not of Hispanic or Latino Origin
NB = 1-6 days old - (Victim Only)	U = Unknown	I = American Indian or Alaska Native	
BB = 7-364 days old - (Victim Only)		A = Asian	U = Unknown
01-98 = Exact age in years		P = Native Hawaiian or Other Pacific Islander	
99 = 99 years or older			
00 = Unknown		U = Unknown	

Victim of Justifiable Homicide - Circumstances	Weapon Used by Offender	
A. Victim Attacked Police & That Officer Killed Victim	11 - Firearm	40 - Personal Weapons – hands, fist, feet
B. Victim Attacked Police & Killed by Another Officer(s)	12 - Handgun	50 - Poison
C. Victim Attacked a Civilian	13 - Rifle	60 - Explosives
D. Victim Attempted Flight from a Crime	14 -Shotgun	65 - Fire/Incendiary Device
E. Victim Killed in Commission of a Crime	15 - Other gun	70 - Drugs/Narcotics/Sleeping Pills
F. Victim Resisted Arrest	20 - Knife/Cutting Instrument	85 - Asphyxiation
G. Unable to Determine/Not Enough Information	30 - Blunt Object	90 - Other
	35 - Motor Vehicle	95 - Unknown

Complete Information for each victim and each offender of this incident only once.

(Use codes above)

*Victim Information: *Offender Information:
(Officer age, sex, race, ethn. is private)

Vic Num	Age	Sex	Race	Ethnicity	Complete Only for Justifiable Homicide Circumstances	Off Num	Age	Sex	Race	Ethnicity	Weapon Used
					For LE Justifiable Homicide enter an "X" for age, sex, race and ethnicity						
1						1					
2						2					
3						3					
4						4					
5						5					

(Attach third page if need to report additional victims, offenders or relationship information for this incident)

VICTIM/OFFENDER RELATIONSHIP CODES

Victim Was : Within Family		Victim Was: Outside Family But Known		Victim Was: Not Known
SE= Spouse (Husband/Wife)	GC=Grandchild	AQ=Acquaintance	XS=Ex-Spouse	RU=Relationship Unknown
CS=Common-Law Spouse	IL=In-Law	FR=Friend	EE=Employee	ST=Stranger
PA=Parent (Father/Mother)	SP=Stepparent	NE=Neighbor	ER=Employer	VO=Victim was Offender*
SB=Sibling (Brother/Sister)	SC=Stepchild	BE=Babysit tee (Baby)	OK=Otherwise Known	*Where all of participants in the incident were victims and offenders of the same offense (double murder, barroom brawl)
CH=Child (Son/Daughter)	SS=Stepsibling	BG=Boyfriend/Girlfriend	HR=Homosexual Relationship	
GP=Grandparent	OF=Other Family Member	CF=Child of Boyfriend / Girlfriend		

*Complete relationship information for each victim to each offender.
(Use codes above)

Victim #	Offender #	Relationship Code
01	01	

*Prepared by:

Title:

*E-Mail:

*Phone:

Agency Head:

(Ex. 2 victims and 2 offenders would require 4 relationships to be completed)

(Attach third page if need to report additional victims, offenders or relationship information for this incident)

* Required Fields   Page 2   Supplemental Homicide Form-R 1/1/2014

SUPPLEMENTARY HOMICIDE REPORT (CONTINUED)

Agency Name:

Case Number:

Additional victim(s) and/or offender(s) of this incident.
(Use codes from previous page)

*Victim Information: ***Offender Information:**

Vic Num	Age	Sex	Race	Ethnicity	Complete Only for Justifiable Homicide Circumstances	Off Num	Age	Sex	Race	Ethnicity	Weapon Used
06						06					
07						07					
08						08					
09						09					
10						10					
11						11					
12						12					
13						13					
14						14					

Additional relationship information for each victim to each offender.
(Use codes from previous page)

Victim #	Offender #	*Relationship Code

*Prepared by:

Title:

*E-Mail:

*Phone:

Agency Head:

(Ex. 2 victims and 2 offenders would require 4 relationships to be completed)

SUPPLEMENTARY HOMICIDE REPORT (CONTINUED)

Terms/Definitions:

American Indian or Alaskan Native - A person having origins in any of the original peoples of the Americas and maintaining cultural identification through tribal affiliations or community recognition.

Asian - A person having origins in any of the original peoples of the Far East, Southeast Asia, or the Indian subcontinent including, for example, Cambodia, China, India, Japan, Korea, Malaysia, Pakistan, the Philippine Islands, Thailand, and Vietnam.

Black or African American - A person having origins in any of the black racial groups of Africa.

Domestic Dispute (Abuse/Violence) - can be broadly defined as a pattern of abusive behaviors by one or both partners in an intimate relationship such as marriage, dating, family, friends or cohabitation. Domestic abuse has many forms including physical aggression (hitting, kicking, biting, shoving, restraining, slapping, throwing objects), or threats thereof; sexual abuse; emotional abuse;

controlling or domineering; intimidation; stalking; passive/covert abuse (e.g., neglect); and economic deprivation.

FBI – Federal Bureau of Investigation.

Fetal Deaths – Should be reported based on New York Law, but are not reported to the FBI and not counted for the FBI UCR Program.

Hispanic Origin – A person of Mexican, Puerto Rican, Cuban, Central or South American, or other Spanish culture of origin, regardless of race.

Human Trafficking/Commercial Sex Acts – Inducing a person by force, fraud, or coercion to participate in commercial sex acts, or in which the person induced to perform such acts(s) has not attained 18 years of age.

Human Trafficking/Involuntary Servitude - Obtaining a person(s) through recruitment, harboring, transportation, or provision, and subjecting such persons by force, fraud, coercion into involuntary servitude, peonage, debt bondage, or slavery (not to include commercial sex acts).

Justifiable Homicide – The killing of a perpetrator of a serious criminal offense by a peace officer in the line of duty; or the killing, during the commission of a serious criminal offense, of the perpetrator by a private individual. Justifiable homicides should be reported under 1a Murder and Non-negligent Manslaughter on this form.

Mercy Killing – Euthanasia - refers to the practice of ending a life in a manner which relieves pain and suffering.

Murder and Non-negligent Manslaughter – The willful (non-negligent) killing of one human being by another. As a general rule, any death due to injuries received in a fight, argument, quarrel, assault, or commission of a crime is classified in this category. Suicides, accidental deaths, assaults to murder, traffic fatalities, and attempted murders are not classified as Murder and Non-negligent Manslaughter. Situations where a victim dies of a heart attack as a result of a robbery or witnessing a crime do not meet the criteria for inclusion in this classification.

Native Hawaiian or Other Pacific Islander - A person having origins in any of the original peoples of Hawaii, Guam, Samoa or other Pacific Islands. The term *Native Hawaiian* does not include individuals who are native to the State of Hawaii by virtue of being born there. Other Pacific Island groups included are Carolinian, Fijian, Kosraean, Melanesian, Micronesian, Northern Mariana Islander, Palauan, Papua New Guinean, Ponapean (Pohnpelan), Polynesian, Solomon Islander, Tahitian, Tarawa Islander, Tokelauan, Tongan, Trukese (Chuukese), and Yapese.

Negligent Manslaughter – The killing of another person through negligence, with no willful intent. Included in this offense are killings resulting from hunting accidents, gun cleaning, children playing with guns, etc. Not included are deaths of persons due to their own negligence; accidental deaths not resulting from gross negligence; and accidental traffic fatalities.

White - A person having origins in any of the original peoples of Europe, North Africa or Middle East.

UCR – Uniform Crime Reporting is a city, county and state law enforcement program which collects crime statistics from local law enforcement agencies and submits data to the Minnesota UCR Program. The State UCR Program then submits to the national UCR Program administered by the FBI.

MORE FROM THE AUTHOR

No Other Man (2011) ISBN-13: 978-1465355355

Redeye (2012) ISBN-13 : 978-1469187242

Forever Your Girl (2012) ISBN-13: 978-1477148952

The Alysè Diaries (2022) ISBN-13: 978-1637651988